About the author

T.J Weekes is a twenty-four-year-old inspiring author, who spends most of her time reading or writing. She has been writing since she was just fourteen years old, and has always wished to see her book turned into a film.

With this dream, she hopes to push her work to the best of her imagination.

THE DRAGON RIDER

T.J. Weekes

THE DRAGON RIDER

Vanguard Press

A CIP catalogue record for this title is
available from the British Library.

ISBN 978 1 78465 486 3

*Vanguard Press is an imprint of
Pegasus Elliot MacKenzie Publishers Ltd.*
www.pegasuspublishers.com

First Published in 2019

**Vanguard Press
Sheraton House Castle Park
Cambridge England**

Printed & Bound in Great Britain

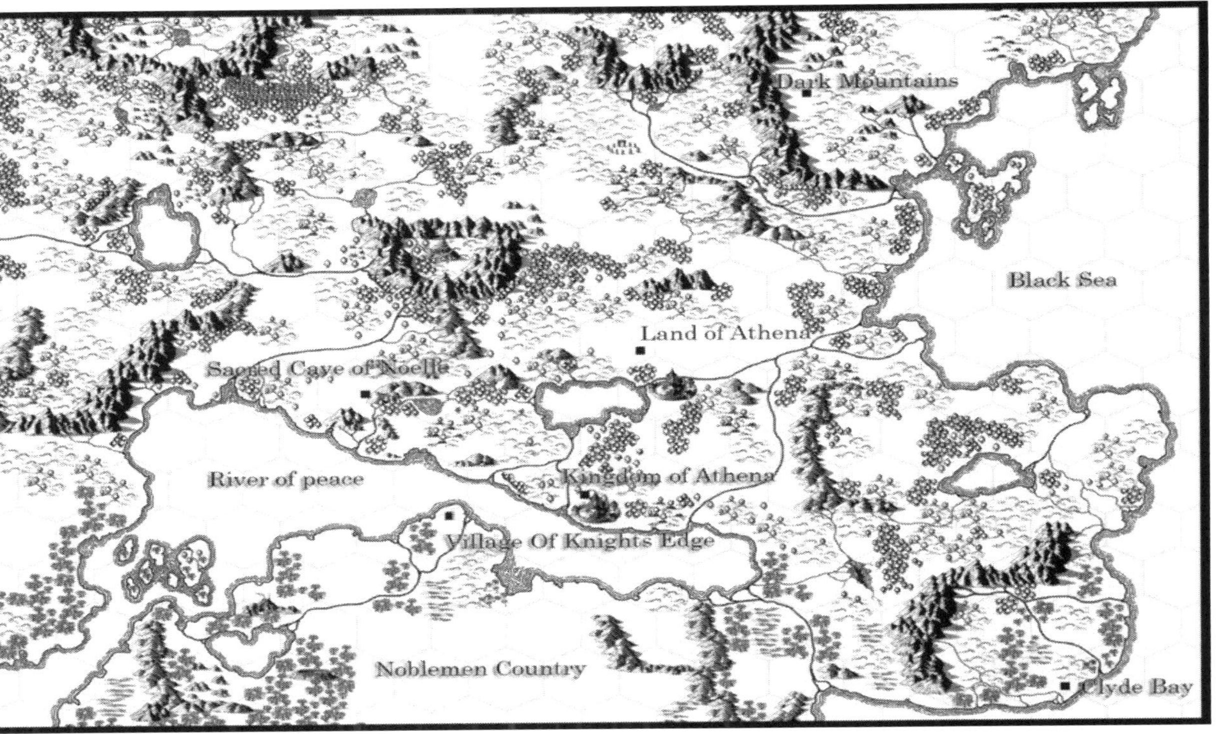

Dark Mountains
Black Sea
Land of Athena
Sacred Cave of Noelle
Kingdom of Athena
River of peace
Village Of Knights Edge
Noblemen Country
Clyde Bay

Dedication

I would like to firstly thank you all for reading my work. It has been a long road to get it here, but without the love and support from those readers online none of this would've happened.

I'd also like to thank my mother and father for their continued support of my work, and for pushing me when I wanted to give up. Without them, I know I would've stopped.

Prologue

Centuries ago, dragons and their Riders were free from any battles. The lands on either side of the twelve apostles lived in perfect harmony and wealth, but all of that changed when a rare dragon egg from the sacred Cave of Noelle was stolen. The egg was the sole life-force that kept the dragons and their Riders connected in ways you could never imagine. The dragons once held great power that would often be channelled through to their Riders. The Riders were able to tap into their dragon's power, with some Riders being able to bend certain elements; but since the egg was stolen, their powers vanished with it.

They were unable to move for days on end as the power drained out of their body – nobody knew where the dragon egg had gone. King Albert from the land of Athena had sent his men on their horses to search all the villages, but nothing was ever found; the egg had simply vanished.

King Albert demanded the people to come forward if they knew anything and even placed coins up as a reward. Many people had come forward with things they had made up, apart from one. A fellow member of King Toban, the ruler of the Dark Mountains, had come forward saying it was the king's men who had carried off the egg.

King Albert immediately sent his men off to the Dark Mountains to confront King Toban, but on arrival for their meeting, they were ambushed. King Toban had sent the fellow member over to the land of Athena in hopes that King Albert would take the bait.

When the men had set foot into the Dark Mountains, they were set upon by rogues. The rogues had outnumbered King Albert's men, who sadly perished. Since then, a century has passed and the dragon egg has never been returned. Hopes of the dragons gaining back their powers had vanished, along with the hope of a mass dragon army.

Since the disappearance, the amount of Dragon Riders has fallen. Only a few Dragon Riders have been chosen over the past few years, and all men had to be trained in the event of an attack.

In the kingdom of Athena, a lone priest would write down each name of the men chosen by their egg to join the long list of Dragon Riders. Never has a dragon left their Rider's side. The men that are destined to become Dragon Riders are fierce men that are willing to risk their own life in order to protect the kingdom they serve under; but most of all their dragons. When a dragon is hurt, their Rider also feels the pain. They are connected in ways we mere humans do not understand.

My mother always told me that the dragons appear to the Riders in their dreams when they are young; but, of course, being a child you only think it is your imagination. All that changes on the day of your eighteenth birthday.

On the night of your eighteenth birthday an egg appears, and that egg is your dragon. Once that dragon has been found by its Rider, it will hatch and leave a marking on its Rider. No two markings have been found to be the same.

Mother always told me that the marking given by the dragon represents the dragon's inner power and ability that it could have had. I always wished I could be a Dragon Rider and often dreamed about serving the kingdom. When I told my mother about my dreams, she dismissed it, since a woman could never be a Dragon Rider. Only men have ever been chosen.

In the history of Dragon Riders, the priests have only ever written down men. People believed that the egg that had been stolen from the Cave of Noelle could have held the key for more Dragon Riders.

When women talked about wanting to be a Dragon Rider, they were mocked and sometimes tortured by their fellow villagers, with some men joining in. The Riders were all self-righteous men that thought too highly of themselves.

The role of a Dragon Rider is to protect the land of Athena and help those in need. It's their duty to be the first line of defence in a war, and they are trained harder than any soldier in the land. If a Dragon Rider fails to help, then the land is bound to perish.

When a Dragon Rider is found, they are put through various challenges to find out what category they fit in. There are two types of Dragon Rider Defence Teams. Fighter Type dragons are the ones that head straight into the battlefield. Strategic Type dragons are the type to fly around as they come up with a plan on how they can take out their enemy. Using these two types of Dragon Defence Teams has seen the kingdom of Athena succeed in many battles.

Men from each village would have the honour of being selected to become a Dragon Rider. The first and only from my village was my best friend, Markus. Our village sits on the side of a mountain, overseeing the River of Peace and the Kingdom. It's a hallowed ground filled with kind and loving people. The name for our village was given to us for our contribution to soldiers and the Dragon Riders. We help provide weaponry and food, and this is why we were given the name Village of Knights Edge.

When Markus was chosen as a Dragon Rider, our village celebrated for days on end. Everyone was so happy that a simple farming boy could be chosen. Markus was a mischievous thing. He was always getting into trouble with the women in the field, but he always had such a big heart. He always loved helping people, and would always help those in need.

Markus was a skinny boy with shoulder-length dark brown wavy hair. He had the bluest eyes I had ever seen. He was so kind to me and always treated me like a princess. When I found out he had been chosen as a Dragon Rider, it broke my heart. To know I was losing my best friend killed me; however, I had to be happy for him. He was perfect to be a Dragon Rider.

The night of his eighteenth birthday, he had been out in the field gazing at the moon when he noticed something shining in the tree-line. After closer inspection, he had found a green egg. The green egg had hatched at the slightest contact of his skin, leaving a marking on the base of his neck.

I hadn't found out about him being chosen until six dragons and their Riders landed in the fields just outside Knights Edge. As soon as I saw Markus walk towards the Dragon Riders, I knew I had lost him. Before he left, he vowed to return to me on the day of my eighteenth birthday, and as that day slowly approached, I grew more and more excited.

Mother had told me he might not remember the promise he made, but I knew he would. He never went against his word, and I knew he never would.

One

It was a bright sunny day in the village of Knights Edge, with not a hint of a fluffy white cloud in the blue sky. Birds whistled as they flew around in the sky, enjoying the day ahead of them. Out in the fields, the farmers were getting ready for the harvest that was soon to come. All the plants looked healthy and rich, and the hopes of a good harvest hung in the air.

Inside one of the many small huts that littered the open field, I was running around looking for my boots. Today was one of the rare days I was not needed in the fields, and I was going to spend it by hunting. Although I still had much to learn, Markus had taught me a few tricks when we went out hunting together. Those days I missed greatly, but the thought of being reunited with him soon filled my heart with joy.

Grabbing my bow that lay beside my nap-sack, I pushed my arm between the gap of the curved wood and the string, so the bow hung off my shoulder. Tying the small arrow bag around my waist, I made sure I had all the things I needed, before heading towards the door.

"Abagail, make sure you're back before supper." Turning round, I gazed at Mother as she tied a small white apron around the lower half of her dress.

Smiling, I nodded. "I will."

Opening the door, I ran towards the tree line, passing a few of the farmers on my way. Running through the forest, the wind ruffled through my long brown hair as I swiped at large trees with a wooden stick. Laughing at the feeling of being completely free, I continued farther into the thick forest on the outskirts of Knights Edge. As I came to a small clearing, I noticed a few birds sitting on a large log not too far from me. Smirking, I grabbed a rock. Tossing it slightly in the air, I caught it in the palm of my hand, before throwing it in the direction of the birds. At the sound of the rock hitting the log, the birds scattered off into different directions.

Shaking my head, I grabbed the bow as I climbed onto the large log. Jumping down, landing in a crouched position, I pulled the wooden bow off my shoulder and grabbed an arrow from my quiver tied around my waist. Lining up the tip of my arrow at a large oak tree where a small squirrel was hanging, I aimed the arrow at the small creature. Releasing my finger, I watched the arrow sail through the air. The sound of the arrow piercing through the oak tree echoed throughout the forest, sending some birds up in the trees flying into the air. Smiling, I jumped up from my crouched position.

"Perfect," I said, as I placed the wooden bow back over my shoulder. Walking towards the oak tree, I bent down to collect my kill. Although it was sad to see such a cute little animal die, I knew this meat would come in handy in the days to come. Putting the squirrel in a small bag around my shoulder, I headed towards my special spot not too far from the village.

Walking towards a clearing in the trees that led to a cliff, I gazed out at the scenery in front of me. Being here was so peaceful. The cliff looked out into the River of Peace and overlooked the kingdom of Athena off into the distance. From here you could see the dragons flying around, as they went about their daily jobs.

Smiling, I sat down on the soft grass below. Just watching the dragons flying about made me yearn to be a Dragon Rider. I would dream about dragons and flying, but I knew I could never be one. I envied the men that were chosen, but most of all I envied Markus. How I wished to be in his place and live as a Dragon Rider. Letting out a sigh, I looked towards the scenery.

As I gazed at the castle, I wondered what he would be doing. Would he be training? Would he be thinking of me like I was thinking of him? Or would he be flying around with his dragon Torren?

Sighing once more, I tilted my head to the side. "I hope you're having fun, Markus," I softly whispered, as I gazed at a dragon off in the distance. Taking a deep breath, a small smile filled my lips.

As I made my way back through the forest, the sound of a twig snapping caught my attention. The forests were full of horrible things, and rogues were the worst. Rogues were horrible creatures that craved for blood. They stood like normal men, but their facial features were like anything but normal. Their teeth were pointed and sharp, and they had blood-red eyes.

People believed that they were once men but were touched by a black healer. Many rumours spread about the rogues, but one story about them was true. The rogues worked for King Toban and often went around tormenting people just for fun. These were the creatures I feared the most.

Stopping in my tracks, I closed my eyes to listen to the sounds around me. Markus had taught me that closing my eyes would allow my hearing to become stronger, allowing me to sense things only great hunters could.

Slowly reaching for my wooden bow and an arrow from my waist, I aligned the end of the arrow up with the string of the bow. Taking a deep breath, I spun around, with my arrow pulled back and ready to shoot.

"Jesus, Alex," I said, as I stared at the person in front of me. Lowering my weapon, I shook my head.

Standing in front of me with a smug look on his face was Markus' older brother, Alex. Unlike Markus, Alex had short brown hair and dark brown eyes. Alex was nothing like Markus, and I was grateful he wasn't. He was a smug man who thought much too highly of himself.

Since Markus left, Alex had looked out for me. He often came to the fields to help me get my work done quickly, but it was always an awkward time with him. Although it wasn't as good as what Markus did, he still offered his help when needed.

Smirking, he crossed his arms. "See, you still have guts. If it were any other woman from the village, they would have screamed their way out of here."

Placing my bow and arrow away, I smiled. "I could have shot you. You do realise that, don't you?"

Shrugging, Alex gave his infamous crooked smile. "I highly doubt a woman could shoot as well as a man."

Raising my eyebrows, I shook my head. "That's what you think," I whispered, before turning round to walk back to the village.

"Hey, wait for me!" Jogging to my side, Alex placed his arm around my shoulder, only to have it shrugged off. Pulling a face, he looked around. "You were looking at the castle again, weren't you?"

"Why? Can I not?" I asked, with a tilt of my head. "It's not against the law of the High Priests, is it?"

Whistling, Alex smiled. "Don't let the High Priests hear that, or you'll be locked up for sure."

Rolling my eyes, I pushed his shoulder. "Sometimes I wonder if you're really Markus' older brother."

Placing his hand on my shoulder, he gave it a gentle squeeze. "Come on, you know I'm the better brother."

Noticing his hand, I took a sharp intake of breath. "Let go, unless you want an arrow through your hand," I said, and, as if my shoulder had suddenly caught fire, he pulled away.

Frowning, he muttered, with a shake of his head, "You know, sometimes I wonder if you're a man in disguise."

I shook my head and smiled. "Come on."

As we reached our village, I grinned at the women working in the field. They all looked really tired, and some of them appeared to be struggling in the sun's rays. My mother was the head worker of the girls and guided them in the harvesting month. It was hard work for her, but there was no other choice. It was the only way we could get coins to buy meat.

Opening the door of our small hut, I noticed that Mother wasn't there.

She must've headed towards the market for food, I thought, as I placed my bow and arrow bag on the floor.

Pulling the dead squirrel from my bag, I placed it on the table for Mother to clean later.

Walking towards a small mat that lay underneath a small window, I rubbed the back of my neck. It was the perfect place to view the moon at night and watch the stars twinkling away. Lying down on the mat, I closed my eyes. A little nap wouldn't hurt. Not too long after my eyes fell shut, sleep overcame me.

Walking around in a dark, damp, misty cave, I looked around for an exit. It was cold and the sound of water dripping from the cave's roof echoed throughout the small space. As I walked deeper into the cave, two small blue eyes off in the distance caught my attention. Squinting my eyes, I pushed away a large cobweb as I made my way closer to the blue orbs.

As I got closer to the eyes, they grew in size as a large dragon's head came into view. A gasp left my lips – the size of its head shocked me. It was bigger than any dragon's head I had ever seen before. Its scales seemed to be a light shade mixed between blue and white. It took my breath away how beautiful this dragon was.

The two horns on the top of its head curved downwards in a graceful way, shaping the dragon's long face. As I gazed at the dragon, I didn't feel afraid, and I strongly felt like I knew it. Reaching a hand out, I went to touch the base of its head, but as my fingers came into contact, it vanished into smoke.

***

Sitting up, I looked around the room. Touching my forehead, it was damp with sweat. The dream felt so real that I was sure I wasn't dreaming. It was as if I was living that moment, and it wasn't just my mind playing tricks on me. I knew what I had dreamt was real, but no one would understand or believe me if I told them.

Walking over to the small bucket filled with water, I splashed some onto my face. As I was looking down at my reflection in the water, the same dragon eyes I had seen in my dream flashed in front of me. As I jumped back from the shock, the bucket of water sailed to the ground, just as the door to our hut opened.

"Abagail, is everything okay?" Mother asked, as she gazed at me.

Swallowing the saliva in my mouth, I nodded. "Yes, Mother, everything is okay. I just tripped, is all."

Nodding, she walked towards the wooden table in the middle of the hut. "I was able to get some meat from the man at the store," she said, as she placed various sizes of meat onto the table.

Standing, I walked towards the basket she had placed down. Pulling out the meat, I softly spoke, "I told you not to go to him. He is not a good man, Mother."

"I know, Abagail," she said. "But we need our food, and if I need to put up with him to get our food, then I will."

"But, Mother..."

"Go wash up," she said, cutting me off. "Food will be ready soon."

Grabbing the knife from the table, Mother went about cutting the meat into bite-size pieces. Sighing for the tenth time that day, I did as I was told. Although I hated her going to that man, I knew there was no other way. My skills weren't as good as the hunters in Knights Edge, and I wouldn't be able to get enough to help both Mother and I. I was only good at catching small animals, not large ones.

Grabbing the small wooden spoon that was placed beside my bowl, I picked up the contents of the soup that Mother had made. It was full of vegetables from the fields, and meat she had gotten today. Food was hard to come by for us, since the farmers didn't get a lot of coins for their work. We had to live off the land, and only ever came across meat when we had enough coins. Mother didn't like me going out into the woods to find food because of what had happened to my father six years ago.

He had left to get food for us to eat, but, as the sun had set, he never returned. Fellow hunters in the village had set out to find him, but all they found were his bow and arrows, which I now use as my own.

Dropping my wooden spoon into my half-eaten bowl of soup, I stared at the contents of the bowl. I missed my father dearly, but no matter how much I wanted him back, I knew he wouldn't return. Mother always told me I looked like him, and as I got older I couldn't help but agree. My eyes and nose were just like his.

"What's wrong, dear?"

Shaking my head, I kept my eyes on the bowl. "Have you ever dreamed of something so real?"

Placing her spoon down, Mother smiled at me. "Why is that, Abagail?"

"I had a dream about the dragon again."

Sighing, she grabbed my hands. "Abagail, they're not real. You know a female cannot become a Dragon Rider. The high priests have only ever written down men."

"But what if times have changed, Mother? What if the day for female Riders is soon to come?" I frantically looked over at her, only to see disappointment in her eyes.

"That's not true." Pulling her hands away, she grabbed her empty bowl before walking towards a bucket of water. "Finish your food and go to sleep. You need to help in the fields tomorrow."

Sighing, I closed my eyes. I was angry that she wouldn't believe me, but most of all, I was hurt. What if the day of male Riders has come to an end and female Riders starts? Just at the mere thought of it, hope filled my heart. I knew I wouldn't be able to convince her of what I was dreaming about, so I stopped any talk of it. Picking up my wooden spoon, I continued eating. By the time I had finished eating the soup, Mother had already fallen asleep.

Quietly getting up from the small table, I placed the bowl into the bucket of water. Once the candles were blown out, I looked around the now-dark hut. The moon was shining through the window, illuminating half of the hut.

Looking out into the woods not too far from our hut, I couldn't help but wish my father would walk back through those trees and return to us. I knew he wouldn't be returning, though. If six years had passed and he hadn't returned, then there was no reason he would now.

Walking towards my nap-sack, I laid down and looked out the small window. The moon was bright, and stars danced along the once-black sky. Smiling up at the moon, the thought of my father played in my mind.

"Wherever you are, Father, I hope you are happy with how much we have grown closer as a family." Smiling, I closed my eyes and let sleep take me.

Two

The sound of dripping water entered my dream, as blue eyes flashed around in my vision. The eyes belonged to a dragon, one that I have often seen in my dreams. The sound of dripping water hitting the ground took over my mind, sending it blank. The eyes flashed once more, before a dragon's mouth came into view, its jaws snapping towards me.

Sitting up in my small nap-sack, I looked around me. The sound of the dripping water was stronger now. Looking around the small hut, I noticed a small drop of water falling from the roof onto the wooden floor, soon followed by another drop.

Pushing my tattered blanket away from me, I walked towards the dripping water. Looking up at the roof, I could see the water forming in the middle, before falling down onto the ground. Sighing, I walked towards a small wooden bucket, placed near the door. Picking it up, I walked back towards the dripping water and rested it on the ground to collect the drops.

The sound of the water falling into the bucket rang louder in the air as the water hit the bottom of the empty bucket. Rubbing my eyes, I looked towards the window near my nap-sack. Outside, the moon shone brightly in the night sky as rain fell heavily.

"Abagail, are you okay?" Mother mumbled.

Turning my head slightly, I could see her lifting her small blanket away from her body.

"I'm fine, Mother."

Nodding, she looked towards the bucket I had just placed down. "Was it raining?"

I sat back down on my nap-sack and nodded. "Yes, it was."

Nodding, she walked over towards the bucket. "Looks like the roof will need fixing." She turned and walked towards me. "Can you ask Alex to help fix the roof when the sun rises?"

I bit my lip and looked down at my hands, which were resting on my lap. Although Alex was a good friend of mine, I still felt uncomfortable around him.

"Abagail?"

"Sorry?" I said, snapping out of my daze.

Smiling, Mother shook her head as she sat down next to me. She placed her hand on my shoulder and gently pushed me back to lay me down. Lying down beside me, Mother pulled me to her side with her hand patting my head in a soothing manner.

"When the sun rises in the sky, please ask Alex to fix the roof for us." Her voice rippled through her chest, the sound calming against my head. Closing my eyes, I nodded my head, before letting the soft hum of my mother's voice send me to sleep.

***

"Will you stop throwing the hay at me, Abagail?" Alex yelled, brushing the loose hay from his short brown hair.

I shook my head and laughed. "Well, maybe if you hurried, then I wouldn't be throwing hay at you."

Alex shook his head, a smirk gracing his lips as he returned to his work. Biting my bottom lip, I looked around the farming area. People were going about their daily work. From the corner of my eye, I spotted something off in the distance. Standing at the edge of the forest, I gazed into the eyes of the very thing that haunted my dreams as a child.

Its dark green skin and blood-red eyes gazed back at me as a sickening grin spread across its face. Before I could stop myself, a loud scream escaped my throat. At the sound of my scream, Alex looked up from what he was doing to see the rogues standing at the forest's edge, weapons in hand. The rogues yelled as they ran forward into the farming village.

As I watched the rogues get closer towards me, a hand reached out, grasping my wrist and spinning me around. "Get your mother!" Alex yelled, before running towards the other farmers. At the mention of my mother, my heart sank. She wasn't near the farming area; she was in the village. Fear filled my body at the thought of her being in danger.

Turning around, I began frantically looking for a horse. Across the way, a dark brown horse tied to a post reared as farmers and their families rushed away from the area. Dodging the other farmers, I ran towards the horse.

I grabbed the reins and pulled them down. Untying them from the wooden rail, I grabbed the horse's mane, before swinging myself onto its back. Kicking the heels of my worn-out boots into the horse, it lunged forward, eager to get away from the scene around us.

Moving the horse back towards the farming area, I spotted Alex fighting three rogues. I knew he wouldn't be able to last for long if he didn't get help soon. Kicking my heels once again, I gritted my teeth as I leaned down to grab a thick branch.

Reaching Alex and the rogues, I swung the branch with a loud grunt, smacking it into the side of a rogue's head, causing it to groan in pain. The horse reared as a rogue swung its flaming torch, startling it.

"Abagail!" Alex yelled, as I fell back down onto the hard ground below.

Grabbing my side, I groaned in pain. I knew just by the pain that I had bruised my ribs, and would need to see a healer if I made it out alive. A yell from above me caught my attention. Standing above me, a rogue held its bow and arrow. The string was pulled back, and as its finger released the string, I rolled to the side, only narrowly being missed by the arrow. Ignoring the burning sensation in my ribs, I grabbed the arrow, before slamming the sharp point into the rogue's foot.

It screamed in pain, as it hopped around with the arrow sticking from its foot. Grabbing the bow that had been dropped, I looked around for Alex, to see him lying on the ground with blood on the side of his face. His face was pale; he lay still. Fear surged through me at the sight. Rushing to my feet, I ran towards him. Kneeling down, I touched his cheek, with my other hand on his chest. With some signs that he was still alive, I sighed in relief as I began gently tapping his white cheeks.

"Alex. Alex, come on, wake up, please." Alex groaned in response, his eyebrows creasing together.

Placing a hand to the side of his head, he groaned once again. "Feels like I was kicked in the head by a horse."

I shook my head before helping him stand. Grabbing the reins of the horse, I pulled it towards me so Alex was able to get on. "Go to the cliff with the other farmers, and make sure no rogues follow you."

Alex frowned as he looked down at me. "I'm not leaving you, Abagail."

"Don't worry about me. Now go!"

Alex shook his head, as he jumped down from the horse. He grabbed my upper arm and began pulling me towards our hut. "I'm not leaving you alone. Get your bow, and we'll go find your mother."

Without a choice, I turned and raced towards the hut. Alex and I dodged the rogues that tried to swing their flaming torches at us, whilst some turned and ran to other villagers that were trying to escape. Grabbing a thick branch from the ground, Alex swung it into the side of a rogue's head, causing it to back away as it cradled its head in its hands.

Throwing the door open, I ran towards my nap-sack. Grabbing my bow and arrow bag, I quickly strapped the bag to my waist. Just as I reached the outside, I gasped as a rogue swung its flaming torch towards me. I ducked out of the way, before rolling onto my side. The pain in my ribs stung from when I fell off my horse, but I knew if I were to let that take priority, I'd have much more to be concerned about than what at this point could just be nothing more than a mild bruise. Grabbing an arrow from the bag, I hastily aligned it with the string of the bow, before aiming. Releasing my finger, I watched as the arrow sailed towards the rogue. A sickening crack echoed through the air, as the arrow pierced its skull. Exhaling in relief, I watched the dead rogue's eyes roll up into its head, before it fell to the ground. My grip on the bow tightened as I ran towards the forest that led towards the inner part of the village, along with Alex.

Jumping over fallen trees and ducking under branches, I prayed to the gods that my mother wouldn't be hurt or dead. Before we reached the inner village, a loud ear-piercing roar echoed around us. Looking towards the sky, I spotted three dragons in all different colours fly past us.

The Dragon Riders were here to help us.

Turning towards Alex, I noticed a big smile on his face. He must have been thinking the same thing. Grabbing my hand in his, he pulled me towards the village. "Come on."

Running into the inner village, I noticed men in armoured suits fighting the rogues, whilst their dragons were picking up the rogues before flying off with them. What they were doing with them I didn't know, but I was just excited to see that we had help.

Rushing towards the market stalls, I frantically looked around for my mother. All I could see were tables turned over, with their contents now lying on the ground. Biting my bottom lip, I raced towards the farmers' stand, hoping and praying that I would find my mother soon.

As I rounded the corner of a hut, I spotted a lady being dragged away by a rogue. My breath caught in my throat at who it was they were taking.

"No," I whispered. "Mother!" I screamed, causing her to look at me.

Never have I seen my mother look so scared. Pulling an arrow from my bag,I pulled the string back, letting the arrow align with the rogue's head. "No one hurts my family." Releasing my finger over the string, the arrow raced towards the rogue, before piercing its skull.

Sighing in relief, I raced towards Mother, enveloping her in a tight embrace. I could feel her shaking like a fish out of water, and it worried me. Pulling back, I grabbed her hand, pulling her towards the safe house.

Rounding the corner of the hut once again, I screamed as a rogue grabbed my arm, pulling me away from my mother. "Let go of me," I said through a clenched jaw.

Unable to grab my bow, I watched as my mother helplessly tried to pull me away.

"Abagail!"

Gritting my teeth, I tried to pull my arm away, but to no avail. The rogue was too strong for me. Just as the rogue had managed to pull me into an empty area a few metres away from the inner village, a loud dragon's scream pulled me out of my thoughts.

Landing on all fours in front of me was a majestic grey dragon, with a man riding on its back. His brown hair was short, with his blue eyes piercing through my own. I felt my heart rate spike just by his looks, but that was short-lived as pain surged through my arm.

The rogue that held my arm had run its dagger along my wrist, letting blood run down to my fingertips. Holding down the scream that wished to make itself known, I tried once again to pull my arm away, until a large shadow fell over us.

The Rider on the grey dragon's back swung his long sword and sliced the rogue's head clean off. I watched as its head slowly fell to the ground, soon followed by its body. I hadn't realised I had been holding a breath until it escaped my lips. Jumping off the dragon's back, the Rider grabbed my arm, his eyes fixated on the cut to my wrist that seemed to keep bleeding. Reaching into his silver trousers pocket, he pulled out a cloth, before quickly wrapping it tightly around my wrist. Looking into his eyes, it was only now that I could see how blue his eyes actually were. They captivated me, unlike any other eyes I'd seen before. I could see his mouth moving, but no words seemed to reach me.

Lifting his hand to my cheek, he gently held my face with his palm. "Are you okay?" His voice was so gentle and full of concern. Opening my mouth to reply to him, I was suddenly pulled from behind into a tight embrace.

"Abagail, you had me so worried," Mother cried. Sighing in relief, I wrapped my arms around her small waist.

"I'm glad I could be of service to you both," the Dragon Rider said.

Mother gasped. Pulling back, she quickly bowed to the Rider in front of us. I was confused as to why she would bow to a Rider. Yes, they were worshipped by many, but I never thought Mother would react like this to one.

"Your Highness, thank you for saving my daughter."

"Daughter?" he asked, with his eyes set on me.

Nodding my head, I remembered Mother's words. "Wait, are you of the royal family?"

Smiling, he nodded. "That's correct. My name is Prince William."

"Oh, no," I whispered. Bowing my head, I kept my gaze on the ground. "Forgive me, Your Highness, I didn't know."

A small chuckle left his lips as he mounted his dragon. The dragon looked down at me, with the same blue eyes as its Rider. It had to have been given to the prince when he found his dragon. As I gazed up at the dragon, a vision of purple scales flashed in my mind.

Moving my head to the side, I closed my eyes. "Darling, are you okay?" Mother asked.

Looking over at the prince and then Mother, I slowly nodded.

"All the rogues are gone, so you are safe now." Prince William smiled as he grabbed hold of a handle on the saddle of the dragon.

Before I could stop my mouth from moving, I quickly shouted out to him. Turning his head so he could see me over his shoulder, I quickly spoke. "There's a man by the name of Markus Dwell. Do you know him? Is he healthy?"

A small smile formed on his lips. "Markus is doing well. In fact, he was here helping me with another Dragon Rider." My eyes widened at his words. Markus was here, and I hadn't been able to see him. "Stay safe, Abagail." With a final glance over his shoulder, I watched as his dragon shot up into the sky, but my mind could only think of one thing right now. Markus.

Three

"Abagail, slow down!" Alex yelled from behind me. Dodging a tree branch, I ignored him as I continued to run towards the cliff just outside the village. I needed to see Markus's dragon. I needed confirmation that he was here and if he was, why he hadn't come to see me.

Lost in my thoughts, I hadn't noticed a tree root sticking up from under the ground, causing my foot to get snagged, tripping me to the dirty floor below. I landed on the ground with a loud thud. Hissing in pain from my wrist, I looked down at the small cloth Prince William had wrapped around my wrist. It was slightly red from my own blood, causing me to panic.

"Are you all right?" Kneeling down in front of me, Alex took my wrist in his hands, causing me to wince from the sudden tug. He released my hand with a frown. "You should go to the healers and see if they can help you."

"I am not going to someone who thinks they have the power to heal. You know as well as I do that those old ladies are just fooling everyone."

Alex sighed at my words. "At least let me take you home. You need to clean that. Who knows what the rogue had used that blade for?" Just at the mere thought of the things it could have done with the blade, I felt bile rise in my throat. Breathing out heavily and giving in, I nodded.

Although I wanted to see Markus dearly, I knew that if I left my wound untreated, my wrist would only become infected. Placing his arms under my armpits, Alex hauled me up to my feet. Looking off into the distance, I could faintly see the cliff. I felt my legs itching to run, but before I was able to, I was lifted into Alex's arms. Frowning down at him, I watched as a smug look crossed his face.

"If you try anything, Alex Dwell, I swear today will be your last living day," I threatened. It's not that I didn't trust him; I just knew what he was like with the other women in the field.

Laughing, Alex shook his head. "You really think…?"

Pulling out my knife from its scabbard, I held it at his throat. He looked at me with eyes full of horror. "What were you going to say?" I asked.

I watched as his throat bobbed up and down; fear had obviously taken over him. "I told you. I may be a girl, but I can still lay you on the ground and beat you. Remember that."

"Yes, it's quite hard to forget when you have a knife held to my throat."

Shaking my head, I placed the knife back into its scabbard. I knew I had gone too far, but I needed him to realise I'm not just any other girl from the village. I was capable of looking after myself. I didn't need someone protecting me.

Once we reached the small hut of my home, I noticed the front door open. I knew Mother was home, cleaning up the mess that the rogues had left. Hell, most of the village had been raided in the attack. Surely, they had done that on the orders of the Dark King Toban. He knew we supplied the Dragon Riders and the soldiers with weapons. Considering that one of the sword-makers was killed in the attack, along with his family, it would take months before we could have the amount of weapons taken replaced again.

Once Alex placed me on the ground, I walked into the small hut. He left to see his mother and father. Apparently, his mother had been injured, but was saved by Markus. At that moment, I wished it had been me saved by him instead.

Pushing the thoughts out of my head, I walked deeper into the hut. "Oh, no...," I whispered. The whole inside of the hut had been destroyed. It was a miracle that it was still standing. The support beam in the middle that held the roof up had been broken, causing it to sit at an odd angle.

Mother stood as she attempted to get the remainder of our things, but I knew from the look of the inside that there couldn't have been much saved. "Mother?" I whispered. A small sob escaped her lips, catching me off-guard.

"Mother, are you all right?"

"The house your father built is destroyed," she said, another sob soon following after as she dropped to her knees. My heart tore at the news. I knew he had helped build it, but never did I realise it meant this much to her. Walking towards her, I was careful of where I stepped. The floor creaked under my feet, obvious signs of the floor struggling under my weight.

Kneeling beside her, I took her hands in mine. Smiling softly down at her, I gently spoke. "The main thing is, we're safe. Father would understand." A tear ran down her cheek at my words. I wasn't sure if I had said the wrong thing, but

I knew I hadn't when she pulled me into a tight embrace, one I hadn't felt since my father's disappearance. Gently stroking her back, I whispered soothing words to her in hopes we could both move on from this disaster.

After several hours of holding my mother, Alex had taken her to his family's hut. We would have to stay there until some of the men in the village could rebuild our hut. Crawling through a small opening in the rubble, I managed to get into what used to be our hut. Tables had been turned upside down, and our food supply lay abandoned on the floor.

Crawling towards the food, I picked up what I could. The Dwell family wouldn't have enough food to go round with the extra mouths to feed now. Although most of the food was uneatable, I still had to try.

Once I had collected all the food I could, I made my way under a fallen plank of wood to get to my mother's sleeping sack. I tied it around my waist and made my way back out of the hut. Being in there any longer would be dangerous.

Once I had arrived at Alex's family's hut, I noticed that their hut was also damaged, but, fortunately, not to the point of not being liveable. Alex's mother, Sarah, picked up a chair before placing it upright. At the sound of new footsteps, Sarah turned around with a sad smile on her face.

"Welcome home." Looking towards me, her eyes saddened. "Abagail." She greeted me with a small nod of her head. Nodding back, I looked around for my mother. Sitting down on a bed roll, head in her hands, I watched as her shoulders heaved up and down. I knew she was upset about the hut, but at least we were alive.

"Abagail," Sarah called.

Turning my attention to her, I watched her smile grow as she looked me over. "The Dragon Riders will be here the day after tomorrow to help rebuild the houses that were lost."

At the mention of the Dragon Riders, I felt a funny feeling in my chest grow. Just the mere thought that Markus would be coming home made me happy. Smiling, I nodded, before heading towards Mother.

Sitting down, I gently placed my hand on her shoulder. Now that I could see her eyes, I could tell she had been crying since she got here. Her eyes were moist with fresh tears, but they seemed to be a little lighter.

"Did you hear that, Mother? Our hut will be rebuilt, and Father would be happy that we could go back home."

Smiling, she wrapped her arms around my shoulder, pulling me into a warm embrace.

***

The very next morning, the village seemed to be busy, rushing around, cleaning and getting things ready for the Dragon Riders' arrival the following day. Everyone seemed to be excited, and some little boys were playing in the streets with wooden swords. I smiled and walked up to them. Bending down, I picked up a wooden sword, before jumping in front of the two boys.

"When a rogue steps out to fight, what do you do?" I asked.

The two little boys looked at each other, before smiling. "We kill them!" they screamed, before rushing at me.

Turning round, I made a run for it, letting the little kids' laughter fill my ears. Rounding a corner, I ran into the busy street of the market. Grabbing hay, I threw it behind me, covering the children as they came up behind me.

"Come back here, you rogue!" one of the boys yelled. At the mention of a rogue, a few of the villagers turned around with shocked faces, before they realised that the boys were playing. At seeing the boys' big smiles, the villagers relaxed as they watched the boys run around after me.

Heading towards the farming section, with the boys still on my tail, I made a quick turn, before hiding behind a building. Hearing their footsteps come closer, I waited for the perfect moment.

"Where did she go?" a boy with light blond hair asked.

Shrugging, the boy with black hair looked around. "Maybe she ran that way."

Smiling, the boys headed in the direction I was hoping for. Once they passed me, I smiled at their little backs. Creeping out of my hiding spot, I picked up the blond boy. His scream pierced my ears before a loud giggle replaced it.

"Abagail!" I heard Mother yell. Looking in her direction, I noticed a smile on her face. Holding up a wooden basket, I watched her smile fall slightly. It had been my day of rest, but due to the attack, no one wanted to work. Smiling apologetically at me, she held the wooden box out to me once more. "Can you go wash these at the river?"

Nodding my head, I placed the blond-headed boy back down. "Sorry, boys, I'll play with you later." Gleeful from our game of pretend, they ran off back into the town, eager to get up to who knows what next.

Running towards Mother, I took the basket from her hands, before quickly placing a kiss on her cheek and rushing towards the river.

The river sat just near the cliff of Knights Edge, before rushing down the side and into the River of Peace. It was a beautiful spot that saw many different plants and fish. The fish were often caught and used at meat stalls, but the plants always seemed to stay. The villagers thought of them as a gift from the River of Peace.

Kneeling down beside the rushing water, I placed the basket down, before pulling out a carrot. Humming a tune my mother used to sing to me as a child, I went about washing the vegetables.

After only washing half, my hands became numb. Shaking my hands free of water, I blew hot air into them, hoping the numb feeling would go away. Looking around the area, I couldn't help the smile that formed on my face. It was so peaceful here and it almost seemed as if no harm could come to this area.

As I continued to gaze around me, something shining in the river caught my eye. It was a light blue colour with a hint of white. It shone just like the stones did that the healers had, emitting a soft warm glow. Walking towards it, I couldn't help but feel myself become mesmerised by its glow. It was almost like it was calling to me, and for some reason I couldn't break out of the trance.

Walking into the river, I stopped just inches away from it. Tilting my head to the side and reaching out, my body wanted to touch the object that had me in such a trance. Just as my fingers touched the top of the glowing object, I was thrown backwards onto the grass of the shore. Landing with a loud thud, I breathed heavily as my body tingled. It was almost like I was shocked, but what had I touched? There were no electric eels in this area. Resting on my elbows, I looked back to where the object was, only to see it hanging in the air, and only then did I realise what it was.

Drifting mid-air was a light blue dragon egg. My breathing stopped slightly as shock ran through me. "This can't be," I whispered.

The egg slowly started to emit the glow it had only seconds before. The glow was so bright that I had to shield my eyes from the egg, before a big gust of wind almost pushed me back further. Once the bright light had disappeared, I slowly lowered my arm. Standing in the river was the biggest dragon I had ever seen.

Its scales were large, in a light blue and white colour, its eyes a dark purple with a hint of blue. Gazing at the dragon, I watched as it lowered its head, as if bowing down to me. "What is going on?" I whispered.

You have found me at last, Abagail.

"How do you know my name?" I asked, as I gazed up at the dragon's face.

It looked as if it was smiling at me. *I know a lot about you, Abagail. I know you lost your father when you were young, and that you have dreamed of me for many years.*

Standing to my feet, I bit my bottom lip. *This can't be real. I must be dreaming again*, I thought.

You're not dreaming, Abagail. My name is Aurora, and you are my Rider.

After her words filled my mind, a burning sensation started to cover my right shoulder blade. Hissing in pain, I closed my eyes as the burning sensation started to become too much for me to handle. Letting a scream leave my lips, I dropped to my knees as I tore the fabric of my worn-out top.

Aurora moved closer to me, enveloping me in her wings. *It will be over soon, my Rider.* Her voice was soft, almost soothing to my ears. After what felt like hours, the burning finally stopped. Breathing heavily, I lifted my gaze up to Aurora. Her purple eyes seemed to glow as she looked down at me.

Turning my head towards my shoulder, I ran my hand along the area where it had moments ago been hurting. Under my fingertips I could feel a rough mark. Furrowing my eyebrows, I looked up to Aurora for help.

That is your mark, Abagail. I have one just like yours in the same spot on my back. Following her gaze, I could see a mark that was a glowing light blue.

"It's beautiful," I whispered.

And so is yours.

"I don't understand, though," I whispered. Looking up at my dragon, I watched as she lay her body on the ground. "Females aren't meant to be Riders. Only males have ever been chosen."

Nodding her giant head, she grinned down at me, causing me to see her sharp teeth.

That is true, Abagail. A new era of Dragon Riders has started... and it's started with you.

Sighing, I shook my head. Opening my mouth, I went to ask another question, but the sound of Mother's voice yelling my name entered my ears, cutting me off.

"I'm sorry, Aurora, but I need you to stay out of sight of the other villagers."

I understand. The other Riders will soon come for you. As soon as I hatched, the High Priests wrote down the name of your village. They will be coming here, and you must let them know it's you. We have much to accomplish together, Abagail.

Nodding my head, I looked towards the tree-line. Just on the other side was my village. Just at the thought of leaving my mother, fear had filled me.

Do not be scared, Abagail. You will be a Rider to defeat the most awful evil known to this world.

"How do you know that?" I asked. Nuzzling her giant head softly against my stomach, I felt my mark tingle.

I have seen our future, Abagail. All dragons do, but we must keep it a secret, as all futures change.

"So if my future changes, can you see it?"

Nodding her head, she looked up at me.

Yes, we can, but only glimpses.

"Abagail!" Mother yelled. She seemed closer now.

"You must stay hidden, Aurora, please!" I yelled, as I ran towards the shore. Picking up the basket, I ran towards the village. Standing just at the tree-line to the forest, Alex was speaking with my mother, who looked distressed.

At the sound of a twig snapping, both their heads looked up in my direction, before Mother's face changed from concern to relief. Pulling me into a hug once I reached her, Mother sighed. "Why didn't you answer me, Abagail? I was so worried the rogues had taken you away from me."

Smiling, I pulled back. "I'm sorry. I had things on my mind. I didn't mean to scare you." Looking to my side, I could see Alex smiling. Smiling back, I nodded his way.

Four

After handing Mother the basket full of now-clean vegetables, I ran to what was left of our hut. Although it had not been repaired, I needed to change my top before anyone could see my mark. Although Aurora told me to show myself when the Riders come for me, I didn't want to do that. After the attack on the village, I couldn't see myself leaving my mother. I could just picture the hurt in her eyes when she found out that I was the new Rider, after all those years of telling me it was impossible. She'd already lost so much of what our family was, between Father and the damage to the hut, how could I tell her she was going to lose me, too?

Biting my bottom lip, I crawled through our hut towards my nap-sack and bag. Inside the old bag were some worn-out and tattered clothes. Rummaging through the bag, I heard the sound of the floorboards creaking, stopping my hand mid-search.

Turning my head slightly, I could see someone walking around in our hut, but I didn't know whose shoes they were. Fear surged through me as my heart rate picked up.

Abagail, what's wrong? Aurora asked.

Not replying, I breathed as quietly as I could through my nose. Slowly bringing my hand out of the bag, I reached down to the knife strapped tightly to my thigh. Pulling the knife out of its sheath, it made a soft clicking sound, causing the person to stop.

Freezing, I waited for the person to move. Watching them bend down to see under the pillar I was currently under, I gripped the blade tighter in my hands. As the person's face came into view, I sighed in relief at who I could see.

"Do you have a death wish or what, Alex?" I said, letting out an exasperated sigh. Condescendingly, Alex bent down a little more, before eyeing the blade in my hand.

"Were you really going to use that?" he asked, pointing to the knife still tightly gripped in my hand.

"If I hadn't recognised your ugly face, then yes, I was going to use it on you. Why didn't you make any sound?"

"Well, I didn't exactly think anyone was going to be in here now, did I?" Tilting his head to the side, that familiar smirk annoyingly graced his lips once more. "What were you doing in here anyway?"

Pointing to my bag, I reached in, before grabbing the top I had wanted. "I was going to change into this."

Frowning, he looked at me. "Why? It's not like the one you're wearing is dirty."

"I know, but I felt like changing. Now, if you don't mind... I would like to change."

Continuing to smirk, he looked me up and down. "I don't mind if you change right…"

Stopping his words mid-sentence, he looked at the blade that had landed inches away from his face, before looking back at me. "You were saying?" I demanded.

Watching his throat move in fear, I waited for a response we both knew was never coming. Placing his hands in the air, I watched him slowly retreat back to the front of the hut. In solitude once again, I closed my eyes and sighed. Fear gripped my chest as I thought back to what had happened earlier by the river.

How was I going to keep this from my mother? Better yet, how was I going to keep it from the town when the Riders came for me? I knew they were coming here tomorrow to help re-build our village, but if the priests put down the town's name, then it meant they would be here before daybreak.

After changing into my new top, I headed back towards the farming area. The women in the fields were working harder than before to save some of the crops. Most of it was destroyed in the attack; although damaged, some of the crops could be saved and taken to town to sell.

Looking around the area, I noticed that my mother wasn't there. Frowning, I walked towards Jessica. Jessica was the second in charge of the women when my mother wasn't there. Bending down to her height, I watched as she picked some of the damaged crops, before placing it into a large wooden crate.

"Jessica...," I whispered.

Turning her head to my voice, I watched as a smile graced her whole face. "Abagail! Just the person I wanted to see."

Frowning, I looked up at her. "Why did you need to see me?"

Jessica wiped her hands on her worn-out apron. "Follow me," she said, as she started to head off in the direction of her hut. Luckily for her, Jessica's hut wasn't damaged in the attack. All she lost were a few plants that were scattered along the front of her hut. Other than that, her hut was relatively unscathed. If anyone were to judge the damage done to the whole town by her hut alone, they'd think the only terror here was the mischievous boys from the market earlier, not a band of rogues.

Walking through the doorway, I stood by the entrance as she walked over towards a small table in the middle of the room. Placed on the table was a small cane basket with a square piece of fabric covering the top.

"Your mother wanted you to go to the local meat stall and swap these vegetables for some meat," she said.

Walking back to me, I reached out for the basket and lifted the fabric off the top. I peeked inside to see what would be my tools of bargaining this time. Mother had left me potatoes, a sprig of herbs, onions, and a handful of carrots.

Gratefully, I smiled up at Jessica. "Thank you for giving me these."

Nodding her head, she sighed. "Just be careful with old man Jenkins, okay? You know as well as I do that he is a sleazy old man."

With a firm nod, I covered the basket once again. Gripping the basket at my side, I thought about old man Jenkins. Old man Jenkins was a fat man with a belly that couldn't be covered. He was always covered in sweat and panted just from moving his small finger. How he was able to become a butcher in the village was beyond me.

"I will be fine. If anything happens, I have my knife," I said. Reaching down, I lifted my thigh to grasp the knife strapped into its sheath. The sheath had been Markus's, but was given to me when he left.

Smiling, Jessica nodded. "Well then, since you seem prepared and ready, I best get back to the girls."

Not knowing when the next time I'd see her would be, I gave her one last glance as I bowed my head and turned to walk back outside towards the tree line. On the other side of the tree line stood the inner village, and where old man Jenkins would be. Just the thought of having to see him made my skin crawl and goose bumps form.

Is everything okay, Abagail? I can sense your worry.

Aurora, I thought. It had been a couple of hours since I had heard from her, almost making me believe that I hadn't met her. Biting my bottom lip, I looked around before speaking. "I'm fine, Aurora. How can you sense what I'm feeling?"

A soft chuckle entered my mind. *I can sense many things from you, Abagail. You and I are tied to each other beyond what you may believe. One day soon, you will fully understand.*

"Why can't you tell me now?" I asked.

Now is not the right time. I can see someone moving to your left.

Looking to my left, I, too, could see a dark shadow moving. Squinting my eyes, I tried to focus on who the person was; however, as quickly as my eyes focused, the figure disappeared into thin air.

"What? How did…?"

Abagail! You need to get to the village now! I can't sense that person anymore!

Heeding her words, I picked up my pace as the sight of the village peeked through the trees. As I got closer to the village, I couldn't shake the feeling of something or someone watching me. Glancing over my shoulder, I tried to see if anyone was there, but it was pointless; I couldn't see anything. The only thing I *could* see was more dense forest, with a few odd animals running around.

As I cleared the forest, I felt relief fill me. Had I really been that scared of something I couldn't see? Or was it the fact that Aurora couldn't sense them which scared me so much? If she had been able to sense them to warn me, I wondered who it could have been in order to just disappear. No one was capable of great magic like that, unless…

"King Toban," I whispered.

I, too, thought the same, Abagail.

"How is this possible?" I whispered.

Many things are possible with the king. Look what happened to the dragon when the egg was taken from the Sacred Cave of Noelle.

She was right. Since then, many strange things had happened. It first started with the rogues. They had once been ordinary men, but since they were touched with dark magic, they turned into creatures of nightmares. I tried once again to focus on my task. I needed to get the vegetables to old man Jenkins, so we had meat on our table.

Since we had more mouths to feed, I needed to try everything possible in order to get as much meat as I could. Rounding the corner of the meat stand, I could see through the small opening. Old man Jenkins was standing behind a large table, with an assortment of meat in front of him.

Walking through the door, I glanced around the room. Hanging from the ceiling on giant metal hooks was a variety of dead animals. One I noticed to be a deer. How he obtained that was beyond me.

"What do you want?" he growled. Turning my head towards Jenkins, I clenched my teeth at his sight. His once white t-shirt was covered in sweat, now staining it to a light brown. Blood marks covered his top as well as his brown trousers. His fat tummy poked out from under the shirt, and the sight of his hairy shoulders and back made me want to throw up.

Swallowing the lump in my throat, I placed the basket on the table. "I want to trade these vegetables for some meat."

Raising his eyebrows, I watched as he leaned on the table, causing some of the meat to touch his shirt. Breathing out through my nose, I made a mental note not to pick that lump of sweat-covered meat.

As I lifted the cover off the basket, I watched as a smirk creased his fat, greasy face. "You want to exchange these for some of the rare meat I have here? This won't do, not at all, no, no, no..." He was tutting and smiling while he shook his head. "Not going to happen. These are only worth a leg of a rabbit. If you want more meat, you'll need to give me something better than this...," he said, gesturing at the basket.

Gritting my teeth, reminding myself of the fact I needed to stay calm, I asked, "And what do you want? What can I give you in order for you to give me meat to cover four mouths?"

Taking a deep breath, I watched as a flirtatious look covered his face. Leaning on the wooden table, Jenkins crossed his arms as he looked at me.

"It's really simple, dear Abagail," he whispered.

Bile rose in my mouth at the mention of my name. In the back of my mind, I could feel Aurora starting to stir. She hated this barrel of lard as much as I did.

Reaching out to me, Jenkins tried to grab my hand, but I only took a step back. "Hurry up and tell me what you want, before I leave."

"All right then. I want your mother."

At the mention of my mother, I felt the air leave my lungs. "You what?" I whispered.

"You heard me. Your mother will become my wife. I want offspring of my own, and since she isn't wed to anyone, she will wed with me."

Gritting my teeth, I felt anger surge through my body. "You really think I would let my mother go to someone such as you?"

"You will do what I say if you want the meat."

Within a blink of an eye, I had reached out, grabbing Jenkins by the collar of his shirt, before placing my knife at the base of his throat. I felt like I wasn't in control of my actions, almost like someone else was.

"Y-Your eyes... they're..." he mumbled, gulping in fright. I watched as the blade moved with his actions. "Purple!" he shouted in fear.

Snapping out of my daze, I pulled the blade away. Grabbing his throat, I watched as Jenkins backed away from the table, his eyes still fixated on me. "The only way you could have those eyes is if…" Stopping mid-speech, he looked towards the door.

"There's no way a woman could be a Dragon Rider."

Sighing, I placed my blade back in its sheath. "Yeah, well, things change. Now, about that meat."

***

As I headed back towards the farming area, I couldn't help the bad feeling that was rising in my chest. I had just had my eyes change colour in front of a member of my village. If the Riders came for me, Jenkins would easily declare me as the new Rider.

Frowning, I shook my head. I knew there was no way anyone would believe him, since it's only ever been men placed as Riders.

Until now.

"Aurora?" I whispered.

Yes, it's me, my Rider.

"I don't understand. I know that the Rider's eyes change once their dragon has been found, but how come mine only changed when I was angry?"

That's because you are different, Abagail. You are not like any Rider out there. For you, you are able to hide your eyes, only tapping into me when you are angry or we are together.

"So what you're saying is that I can hide the fact that I'm a Rider?" I asked, as I tightened my grip on the basket's handle, causing its splinters to dig into my palm.

Yes, that's correct. You will only ever change when with me or when you need my strength.

53

"So me being able to move that quick was me tapping into your strength?"

Yes

Five

Arriving at the river, I thought to myself how tranquil this scene was. With the sound of rushing water entering my mind… it was so peaceful. In contrast with the past few days' events, it seemed strange that such a place, such a break in the world, could exist. I looked around for Aurora, gripping my bow slung over my shoulder, just in case. Not seeing her, I decided to see if she would show when I whistled.

With the sound of air being pushed through my lips, the cracking of branches caught me off-guard, before Aurora appeared in the sky above, flapping her wings as she rose from the forest. She had stayed, just like I had asked her to. Landing on her hind legs, Aurora gracefully placed her front legs down, before folding her wings elegantly behind her. In the setting sun, for the first time, I realised what a majestic creature she truly was. Her blue-white scales seemed to shine like diamonds as her blue eyes melted away any sense of fear and dread I'd been feeling.

Abagail. Aurora spoke, dipping her head low in respect.

I began walking closer to her. Slowly raising my hand, I gently placed it against the side of her head. This was the first time I'd ever felt the surface of a dragon. The texture was rough against my smooth skin, and up close the scales seemed to look more defiant. Each scale seemed to be tougher and more hardy than the next, indicating that she wouldn't go down easily.

Moving closer to the side of her body, I gazed at her shoulder where the mark stood. There, on her back, was the same mark that I had on my shoulder-blade. It looked like a dragon's tail, curving slightly at the top, from which pointed horns followed all the way down from tip to tip.

It means strength, Aurora whispered. Her head gently nudged my side, causing a smile to form on my lips.

Turning towards her, I gazed into her bright blue and purple eyes that were just in front of mine. "How do you know what it means?"

Each Rider bears a different mark, all meaning something different. To other dragons, it shows who you belong to and what that person represents. Her head lowered slightly before she moved, so her body was surrounding mine. Working like a cocoon, she used her body so I could lay against her. Placing her head on my lap, she continued.

You, Abagail, show so much strength, carrying it with you every day.

"Me?" I asked, bewildered. "How do I show strength? All I do is pretend to be strong; there is no way that this mark means that."

Breathing through her nose as if she had scoffed, Aurora gently nudged my head with her own.

See, that's where you are wrong, dear Rider. Strength comes from the heart. You have shown so much of it when protecting your family and loved ones.

Looking down at my hands that rested on my lap, I mulled over her words. Yes, I showed strength when it was needed, but I couldn't get myself to believe in what she was saying.

"How can I show strength when every time I get close to someone they leave?" I whispered.

But that's where you are wrong, Abagail. No one ever fully leaves; they always stay with you in your heart.

She was right. Even though my father had disappeared, I still thought about him every day and carried his bow and arrows. I knew that he would be proud of whom I have become; and that he was smiling down at me right now.

That's what I wanted to hear, Aurora whispered. *Just remember, strength is from the heart, not the head.*

Satisfied, I stood up and onto my feet. I felt like a weight had been lifted off my shoulders. I knew something about my mark, and now I wanted to know some more. There was still so much that I needed to know and I had a long lesson ahead of me.

"Tell me about dragons," I said, looking up at Aurora.

Well, each dragon looks different. No dragon looks the same. We all have different markings, as you know, and we can only speak to our Rider. No other Dragon Rider can hear our thoughts.

"Wait, so you're only thinking what you want to say?" I asked.

Yes, that's correct. Our roar is us using our voice, she chuckled.

Smiling, I shook my head. Turning round, my smile grew. "I want to fly."

Taken aback by my sudden declaration, Aurora stood on all fours.

Isn't that a bit risky when you don't have a proper riding saddle?

Shaking my head, I moved closer towards her. "I have to ride one day; and besides, it's not like I can just bring one down from the horsemen. They won't exactly fit you; you're bigger than normal dragons."

Chuckling in my mind, Aurora laid on her stomach.

Step onto my wing, she said.

Doing as she asked, I stepped onto her wing, only to have her lift them, causing me to wobble at the sudden action. Using it as a platform, I crawled onto her back. Now that I was sitting on her, I couldn't help but feel dizzy. I was a lot higher than I had thought, causing me to bite my bottom lip.

As Aurora stood onto all fours, I grasped around her neck. "Easy now," I whispered.

I said it was risky, she replied. *How about we just walk for now?*

Nodding my head, my grip tightened around her neck as she took a gentle step forward. Being on her back felt surreal. It was like all my dreams were coming together, to make this feel like it, too, was just another dream that I could wake up from.

"What's going to happen when the other Riders come with the High Priests?" I asked.

Crossing the running river, Aurora walked deeper into the forest. *Nothing bad will happen.*

"But what if it does? What happens if they refuse to take me as a Rider?" I questioned.

Then we show them just what we're made of. With that, she let out a loud roar, scaring some birds out of their trees and into the night sky. *You have amazing fighting skills, Abagail, and with my strength, you can do wonders.*

Lifting my head from on top of her neck, I gazed down at her face. "You'll stand by me, won't you?"

Always.

With that, she shot up into the air with a loud whooshing sound. Gripping on to her neck tighter, I watched as the buildings from the village became nothing but little specks as the clouds covered us.

"Please don't let me fall!" I yelled.

I would never let you fall, Abagail. Just hold on tight.

Angling her wings, she dived down towards the ground. The feeling of air escaping my lungs caught me off-guard as a tingling sensation filled my chest. Not being able to control myself, laughter escaped my lips. I loved this feeling. I felt free and knew that I finally had my own duty in life.

Let's take this a little lower, she laughed.

Continuing closer towards the ground, I watched as the clouds soon vanished and the tops of trees travelled closer and closer towards my body. Closing my eyes, I braced myself for the impact of the ground, but the sensation of falling vanished and was replaced with calm floating.

I told you I would never let you fall, Abagail. Now open your eyes and look around.

Opening my eyes, I gazed at the beautiful scenery in front of me. We were flying over the River of Peace. Keeping an arm wrapped around Aurora's neck, and just above the water, I bent down slightly, letting my fingertips touch the cold water.

"This is beautiful," I whispered.

Placing myself back onto her back, I loosened my grip. The river was lit from the full moon above, making the water sparkle. A calm feeling filled my chest as the sight of the Kingdom of Athena came into view. The castle was well lit from torches placed around the outskirts of the kingdom, as lights from inside the castle shone brightly.

One day soon, you and I will be there, Aurora whispered.

At the mere thought of soon being there, I couldn't help but feel scared. I would be leaving my mother all alone. How was I going to walk away from her when the Riders come? All I could picture was the sadness and horror on my mother's face as I imagined turning away to leave her.

"Take me home... please," I whispered. I could feel some tears starting to well in my eyes.

As you wish, my Rider.

***

Landing back on the empty field, I was quick to jump off Aurora's back, before heading back towards the hut. I didn't want her to see my tears. I knew she had sensed my distress over leaving my mother, but I was thankful that she hadn't tried to stop me as I left.

Once I cleared the forest and made it into the farmers' area, I looked around. There was still some damage from the rogue attack, and a few of the huts stood empty, along with our own. Walking closer to the hut, I gazed at its front.

"I'm sorry, Father," I whispered. "Please stand by me in my decision."

Lowering my head, I felt a tear fall. Clenching my fists, I took a deep breath to steady my shaking heart, before heading back towards Alex's hut. As I got closer, I heard talking. Standing outside were a few of the farming families and some people from the inner village. They were all looking inside the hut like something exciting was happening.

Pushing my way through, I walked into the hut to see Mother, Sarah, and Alex all sitting around a table – but what caught me off-guard was old man Jenkins.

Old man Jenkins was sitting at the table like he owned it. He was still wearing his clothes from earlier that day, only causing my irritation to grow. Mother had her head down, and Alex looked like he was about to kill Jenkins. Walking deeper into the hut, I noticed it became deathly silent.

"What's going on?" I asked.

Looking around at the people behind me, I noticed their eyes avoiding mine. Gazing back at the table, I watched a disgusting smirk form on the old man's lips, as he wiped the sweat from under his chin.

"Your mother is going to be marrying me," he said in a sickly sweet voice.

Shocked, I looked towards Mother. She still had her head down, which only made my anger grow. "Like hell she is!" I spat through gritted teeth. "Get out," I growled.

Continuing to smirk, old man Jenkins stood from his chair. Sarah also stood from her chair, causing it to creak on the wooden floor. "Now, now dear Abagail. Is that anyway to talk to your new father?" he whined.

I watched as he moved around to stand next to Mother, before he placed a hand on her shoulder. Breathing heavily through my nose, a new-found strength and anger coursed through my veins.

"I said, get out!" I screamed.

Grabbing my knife strapped to my thigh, I ran at old man Jenkins. Gripping his neck tightly, I threw him onto the ground, before pushing my knife against his throat. I watched as he struggled for breath like the fat pig he was. I enjoyed watching him struggle beneath my hold, as all my anger seemed to radiate off me.

"Abagail, no!" Mother shouted.

The sound of running footsteps entered the hut as people tried to pull me off Jenkins; but I wasn't budging. Digging the blade of my knife deeper into his throat, I watched as specks of blood formed and rolled down the side of his neck.

"Abagail, get off him!" I heard someone scream, before arms were placed around my waist, and I was hauled away from him. Dropping my knife, I kicked and thrashed as I watched Jenkins get off the ground.

"You!" he yelled, as he gripped his throat. "She needs to be locked away!" he screamed.

Sarah rushed towards me, blocking my view of Jenkins. Covering my eyes with her hands, I felt her cheek press against mine, before her voice softly whispered into my ear, "You need to disconnect from your dragon, Abagail. Don't let anyone see your eyes, please."

Stopping my thrashing, I took a deep breath. The arms around my waist tightened, as I tried to calm myself. Once the feeling of Aurora's strength left me, I opened my eyes, to see Sarah's smiling face in front of my own. "Good girl," she whispered.

Placing a kiss on my cheek, she stepped back. Lifting my gaze back up towards old man Jenkins, I noticed him looking at the blood on his hand. "Leave," I whispered, just loud enough for the people in the hut to hear. "Now."

Grunting, Jenkins pushed himself off the wall, before side-stepping away from me and out the door. The feeling of the arms around me loosened, and without them, the sudden feeling of loneliness filled my body. Gazing at Mother, I noticed how she kept her eyes on the floor as if that was more interesting to look at than me.

"Why?" I asked, defeated.

Sniffling, I watched as mother took a deep breath. "We need food, Abagail."

"That doesn't mean you need to agree to marry him!" I yelled.

"Calm down, Abagail," Alex whispered, as he gripped my arm.

Pulling my arm from his grasp, I walked towards Mother. Pulling her towards my body, I watched as her gaze still fell on the floor. "You won't even look at me and say it. Why?"

"I'm trying to protect you," Mother whispered.

"I don't need protecting! I'm eighteen now, Mother. I can protect myself, and you know I can!"

"Abagail," Sarah gently called, "let's discuss this in the morning, hm?" Sighing, I looked away from my mother. I was angry, and it felt like I couldn't breathe. Walking out of the hut, I headed towards our own. I didn't want to stay with Mother tonight. I wanted to be surrounded by things my father built, where I knew he'd be watching over me.

Opening the door to the hut, I noticed that some of the insides had been fixed. Although the support beam still stood at an odd angle, most of the rubble had been removed. Walking towards my old sleeping station, I sat down. Placing my back against the wood of the hut, it felt nice to close my eyes.

Know that she was only looking out for you, Abagail, Aurora whimpered.

"Not now, Aurora," I said.

I didn't want to hear reasoning from anyone right now. I wanted to be left alone with my thoughts. Resting my head against the wall, I let my body relax as I thought about what would happen when the sun rose tomorrow morning. The Riders were meant to be coming here to help rebuild the village, but would that also mean they would take me, too? How was I meant to leave, now that old man Jenkins wants my mother for himself? What if I left and came back to find my mother with him? What would I do then?

All these questions ran through my mind as I tried to forget about everything. Tonight I just wanted to be left alone, to dream of a better tomorrow and a better life, where old man Jenkins wasn't going to take my mother away from me.

Six

I was already out in the fields working when the sun had begun to rise the next morning. I had put it upon myself to act like it was just another day. I didn't want to think about the Dragon Riders that were planned to arrive today, nor about the fact that my mother and old man Jenkins could possibly be getting married.

Squatting down to the ground to pull out a weed, I noticed that the area seemed to be very quiet. It was strange that no one was around, but then again I knew it was still very early in the morning and most of the villagers would also be getting ready for the Riders' arrival.

As I placed a carrot into one of the cane crates that I had brought out from the farmer's shed, the sound of hooves hitting the ground echoed around me. It wasn't just the sound of one horse, it was the sound of many.

They have arrived, my Rider, Aurora whispered in my mind.

At her words, I felt my heart drop. I didn't want to face them; and even if I did, I wasn't ready to. Ironic. Only days ago, I desperately wished more than anything to be a Dragon Rider, yet here I stood, shaking and afraid they would find me.

Grabbing the cane crate, I made my way towards the farming shed. However, I came to a sudden stop when the king's horsemen came riding through the farming village. As I watched the men ride past me, I noticed they were all wearing armour and carried the royal flag of the king.

On the flag was a symbol of a gold phoenix on a white cloth. On the border of the flag was a light gold print. In the midst of the men was the king himself, seated on top of a white horse. He was quite easy to spot, dressed in gold armour, which contrasted quite well against his men's silver armour.

As I gazed at the king, I couldn't help but notice how his son seemed to resemble him. They both had the same nose and jaw, but where the king had brown eyes, his son had blue. I wondered if William got his eyes from his mother or his dragon.

Moving my gaze behind the king, I spotted the Priest. A gasp left my mouth at the sight of the Priest and the book in his arms. The leather book with gold around the edges was the same book that had held centuries of Riders' names. That book was what would have my name in it.

Dropping the crate, I gazed at the book as they disappeared down towards the inner village. Once they were out of sight, I felt my heart drop.

Breathing hard, I stared at the ground below me, too afraid that if I looked up, I'd have to face reality. A loud thud on the ground in front of me had me flinching. I closed my eyes and tried to control my breathing.

You do not have to be afraid, Abagail, for I will not let any harm befall you.

Lifting my head towards the sky, I took a deep breath. Pushing the air out of my lungs, I opened my eyes to gaze up at Aurora. Her eyes seemed to hold so much respect and support, and that made me grateful.

"I'm trying to do what's right," I whispered.

Then do it by showing them what we are destined to do.

Releasing a loud roar into the air, Aurora stood on her back legs with her blue wings spread out wide. The show of power not only radiated out of her, but also flowed through me. Smiling up at her, I nodded my head.

"Promise me you will help me every step of the way."

I will never leave you, little one, she whispered.

Looking back at my broken hut, I bit my bottom lip. Father would want me to go and fulfil my destiny as a Dragon Rider; and just by the mere thought of him, I knew he would be proud of me.

"All right," I said. "Let's go show them what we're really made of, then."

Roaring once more, Aurora shot up into the sky. Grabbing my bow and arrow quiver from inside the hut, I ran towards the inner village where I knew everyone would now be gathered.

"Don't appear until I say so, Aurora," I thought in my head.

As you wish, my Rider, whispered Aurora.

Running through the forest, I could feel the power Aurora admitted pulsing through me. Picking up my speed, I made my way towards a fallen tree, before jumping over it and landing perfectly on the ground again. Smiling at the new feeling, I pushed myself to run faster towards the village.

The sound of wings flapping above me had me looking towards the sky in panic. As I gazed up at the sky, I noticed about five different dragons, all of different shapes and colours, flying above me. "Dragon Riders," I said aloud.

Watching as they flew ahead of me, I slowed my pace as I came closer to the inner village. Stopping just outside the village, I watched as many people began to crowd around the once empty field. It seemed like all the village had turned out to watch as the king and his Riders arrived to help us, and all seemed unaware of the real reason that they had all shown up.

The villagers all cheered as the dragons landed on the field, with some of the villagers running towards them as if they were gods sent from heaven. As I watched the Riders jump down from their dragons, I took note of each person.

One man seemed quite short. He had long curly hair, with a chubby build. The armour he wore seemed to make him look bigger than what he possibly could be. Another man was of normal height, maybe around six feet. His hair was short and blond. Round his waist was a sword, its handle glimmering in the morning sun as he jumped down from his dragon.

But what caught my eyes was the person beside him. Prince William. He was dressed in a very well-designed suit of armour, no doubt to protect him more so than the others, as the clothes underneath were of a dark silver. His brown hair had been tossed around from the wind, but he still looked so handsome.

Making my way out of the forest, I watched as more of the villagers approached the Riders. As I got closer, I kept my eyes on William. As if sensing my gaze, his eyes soon locked with mine. Even though women and children were begging for his attention, he still only looked at me.

Bowing his head slightly, I watched as a smile graced his face, causing me to smile in return. Looking around at the villagers, I noticed Markus and Alex's mother crying. Running towards her, I worried that something had happened.

I grabbed her upper arm, pulling her closer towards me. "Is everything all right?" I asked, slightly puffed from running. Biting her bottom lip, she looked back at the Riders, before looking at me.

I watched as more tears filled her eyes. "He's finally home," she whispered, and smiled. Freezing at her words, I watched as her eyes glanced back towards the Riders. Finally, it dawned on me why she had suddenly started crying. Markus was back. Spinning around, my eyes came into contact with the very blue eyes I had missed for so long. His once shoulder-length hair was now cut short and I couldn't help but notice how grown up he looked since the last time I had seen him.

Moving my eyes down his body, I took note that he was wearing green-coloured clothes under his silver armour. His body seemed to be made of stone as the muscles on his arms flexed as he moved towards us.

I was so shocked to finally see him again, I couldn't make any words. Smiling down at me, his blue eyes danced with joy as he looked over my face. "It's good to see you again, Abagail."

Not being able to control myself, I launched myself at him in pure happiness. As I wrapped my arms around him, I could feel his chest rise through the armour as a laugh escaped his lips. The feeling of his arms around my waist made me blush, but that was short-lived, as the king's voice boomed through the open land.

"Ladies and gentlemen, thank you for your hospitality."

Releasing my arms from around Markus, I moved back so I could see the king. Standing next to him was William, a smile gracing his lips as he looked out over all the faces in front of him.

"When I had heard of the rogues entering our land, I sent my Riders straight here in order to protect you. Unfortunately, my men didn't get here in time, it seems," he said, gesturing around to some fallen huts.

Looking through the crowd of people, I spotted Mother moving towards Sarah. Gazing at me, she smiled sadly, before looking towards the king. I then joined her in giving the king our undivided attention.

"I have brought with me my men to help rebuild the homes for those who are now left without one. But that isn't the only reason we have come," he said.

Looking towards the Priest, I watched as he walked towards the King. Bowing in a sign of respect, he held the book in the air.

"We have the name of a new *Rider*!" he yelled. The crowd murmured amongst themselves, all seeming to wonder at who the new Rider was. The feeling of my heart dropping had me closing my eyes.

The feeling of someone lacing their hand through mine caused me to snap my eyes open. Following the person's hand, I looked up to see that it was Sarah who had gripped my hand. As if sensing my eyes on her, she gave my hand a loving squeeze. I knew just what she was trying to tell me.

You are not doing this alone, Abagail, Aurora whispered.

She was right. I would have Markus there to help me and Aurora, too. I took a deep breath and faced the front again, ready to face my future.

"Inside this book is the name of the new Rider who will be joining us, and aiding the kingdom in the quest for peace." Lowering the book back down, the Priest opened the book to the page that was marked with a golden ribbon.

As I gazed at the Priest, I watched his face contort with confusion. "This can't be true," he whispered. "I'm sorry, but there isn't a name in the book."

"What nonsense are you spouting?" Moving towards the Priest, King Albert reached for the book, only to have it moved away.

"Your Highness, honestly there isn't a name here." Panicking, the Priest took a step back. "We should all leave."

The sound of a dragon's roar echoed through the open field, causing the king to look back at the Dragon Riders. "Was that from your dragons?"

Shaking their heads in response, a few of the Riders whispered amongst themselves. Frowning, the king turned towards the forest. "Show yourself!"

With teeth clenched, I closed my eyes. "Do it," I thought. The sound of trees cracking echoed from deep inside the thick forest. Shooting up into the sky, Aurora's large body blocked out the sun as she flew over the top of us. Gasps echoed throughout the field as the king turned to glare at the Priest.

Landing on all fours behind the other Riders, Aurora spread her wings wide in a show of dominance. A few of the Riders gripped their swords as the king moved towards Aurora. As she lowered her body in respect to the king, I nervously watched as King Albert stopped in front of her.

"Give me the book," he demanded, gesturing at the book. I watched as the Priest lowered his head. He placed the book in King Albert's hand. The king flipped it open to the marked page. "Go to your Rider, dragon," he ordered.

Nodding her head, Aurora headed my way. Giving my hand a gentle squeeze, Sarah moved away. Stopping in front of me, Aurora lowered her body.

"Abagail Stone," said the king.

Gasps ripped through the crowd as they all turned to look at me. Beside me, I watched as Markus moved to get a better look at me. Biting my bottom lip, I moved towards the king. As I finally stepped into the clearing, I watched as everyone seemed to judge me with their eyes.

"There's no way this girl is a Rider," the short man said. Some of the other Riders seemed to agree.

"The book never lies," the king stated. Walking towards me with a warm smile, the king placed a hand on my shoulder. "Our new Rider is a female. Abagail Stone, welcome to the Dragon Riders."

Seven

The king's words echoed through my head, as the murmurs of my fellow villagers began to grow in volume. I could hear their shock; but most of all, I could hear the disappointment as husbands spoke to their wives. Closing my eyes and clenching my hands, I took deep breaths to calm my beating heart.

"She doesn't deserve to be a Dragon Rider!" a male's voice yelled. Snapping my head in the direction of the man's voice, anger seeped through my veins. The feeling of new power etched its way through my muscles as they itched to start a fight.

Taking a step forward, King Albert tilted his head at the man. "And who are you to say who can be one of my Dragon Riders?"

Puffing out his fat chest, old man Jenkins smirked towards me. "I'm her new father."

"Over my dead body," I hissed. I felt my vision intensify, as colours seemed to become more enhanced than they were before. Everything around me was bright, with the corner of my vision blurred slightly. Aurora's loud scream ripped through the air as she stood on her back legs, wings stretched out wide in a show of dominance over him.

Pointing his finger at me, I watched as a bead of sweat trickled down the side of his face.

"See what I mean!" he yelled. Taking a step back, I watched as he moved towards my mother. Without giving the command, Aurora moved her wing, shielding my mother from the vile man. Jumping in shock, old man Jenkins clenched his fist.

"Abagail, stop!" Sarah yelled. Pushing the wings out of her way, Mother ran towards me.

Gripping my hands that were clenched tightly by my side, she gently squeezed. "Abagail," she whispered. "You don't have to do this. If you don't want me to marry him, then I won't, I promise you."

Blinking away the new-found vision, I watched as the bright colours faded away into normal colours. I kept my gaze on Jenkins in case he decided to try and do something else stupid.

"Abagail," the king said, "I am unsure of what has caused this anger towards this man, but I assure you, if this man is causing your mother any issues, we can take measures in order for her to stay safe."

Looking down at the ground, I took a deep breath. "I'm sorry," I whispered. Sensing someone to my right, I moved my gaze, to see Markus smiling down at me.

Placing his hand on my shoulder, he gave it a gentle squeeze. "It's okay, little one, you still don't know how to control your feelings yet. All will be explained back at the castle."

"I can't leave yet," I said, looking around at the villagers. I could see so many familiar faces that I had grown to love, and some to hate. "These people have lost homes, family members and friends... I can't leave them when there are still plenty of things that need to be fixed."

"That's okay. We don't have to leave just yet. We will be staying here till nightfall tomorrow, then we head back. You have training to start, and I'm sure your father would want you to start your destiny as a Dragon Rider," Markus said, as he whispered the last part near my ear.

He is right, Abagail.

"Fine." Looking towards the villagers, I said, "I will go with you, but not until the village has been fixed."

A few of the farming ladies smiled my way as children ran towards the dragons. I couldn't help but feel a new sense of hope. Hope for a new start. Hope for my mother. She would finally be able to be protected and knowing that the king would help me stop Jenkins from getting near settled my anger.

After swearing to the king that I would follow him and the Riders back to the castle, the rebuilding of our town was finally underway. Jenkins had been sent away by the king, saying he wasn't needed. Knowing that I wouldn't have to see him made my mood a little better, but knowing the one person I had longed to see was here had my heart soaring into the clear sky.

Markus was a few feet away from me, talking to some soldiers, instructing them on what needed to be done. As if sensing my gaze, he lifted his eyes to meet mine. Mouthing a hello, I watched as he smiled and turned back to the men. I took a deep breath to calm my nerves.

Prince William had taken a few of the villagers to the market area. He wanted to know what provisions needed to be replaced. In the attack, a lot of our harvest was lost, meaning there wouldn't be enough food to go around.

One of the Dragon Riders, a short tubby man, was hacking away at one of the trees. Rising to my feet, I made my way towards him. Sensing my presence, his dragon tilted its head down at him.

Hello, new Rider.

Stunned, I stared wide-eyed at the dark green dragon. "What did you say?" I asked.

Turning from the tree, the Rider frowned at me. "I didn't say anything, lac." He spoke with an accent I couldn't quite pin. He sounded to be from Noblemen Country. Everyone from that area had a strange accent.

"Your dragon just spoke."

"What are you talking about? I'm the only one that can hear his thoughts." Frowning, he shook his head. "I don't understand why the prince or the king wants you to join us," he mumbled.

Looking back at the dragon, I watched in fascination. Why could I hear its thoughts? When the Rider moved back to chopping the tree, I turned my attention back to the dragon. "You can hear me?" I whispered. Tilting its large head, it gazed down at me. After a few minutes with no reply, I shook my head. "I must be hearing things."

After a few hours of working in the fields, the sun had finally found its peak in the sky. To say it was hot was nothing less than an understatement. While a few of the villagers decided they would have a break and head to the market area for food, I, on the other hand, needed some quiet time as I still needed to process everything that had happened.

Sitting alongside the small riverbank, I gazed down at my cut hand. It had healed rather quickly, from what I could only guess was all due to Aurora's healing. I looked out in front of me and sighed, before the sound of an off-note in the forest caught my attention.

Growing up, Markus had always taught me about the sound of the forest and how it always stayed the same. You were always able to pick up if someone was in there, as the tune of the forest would change.

Gripping the dagger strapped to my thigh, I clenched it in my hand. When I knew the person was close enough, I quickly turned to the side, kicking the person down to the ground. Straddling the person's waist, I placed my dagger at their throat; but a small scream released from my mouth when I gazed down at the blue eyes below.

"Markus?" I whispered.

Smiling at me, his eyes shone with admiration. "Good to see my words have stayed in your head, Abagail."

Laughing, I got off him. "Why would you sneak up on me?"

"I didn't sneak up on you; I made a noise," he said.

Shaking my head, I watched him sit up. "Yes, but I thought you were a rogue. I could have killed you."

Shaking his head, his eyes softened slightly. "You wouldn't have."

I turned my body towards the river. How long had it been since we were both sitting here? How long had it been since I had last seen him? "It's been a while," he whispered.

Smiling, I nodded.

"It has, hasn't it...?"

Turning my head slightly towards Markus, I studied him. He had grown up so much from the young teenage boy I used to know. Even though he was three years older than me, I didn't seem to feel the age gap with him, where I did with his brother.

I looked over his form, dressed in royal uniform: he had become a lot more masculine, and the tiny dragon scar stood out on his neck. Without realising what I was doing, I reached over to touch his mark, causing him to flinch slightly.

"So this is what your mark looks like," I said. Pulling down the neckline of his shirt, I studied the pattern. It was of two wings spread wide, as if showing its dominance over anyone who dared to oppose him.

Grabbing my wrist in his hand, he frowned. "You should never touch a Rider's mark, Abagail."

"What do you mean?" I was confused. I thought Riders would be willing to show the mark off to other people, not wanting to try and hide it.

"Back when the war started, anyone that was captured, along with their dragons, had their mark cut out of them. The other Riders knew some people it happened to, so it's not in your best interest to touch other people's marks."

Frowning, I looked towards the ground. "I'm sorry," I whispered. I hadn't meant to offend him; I just thought it looked beautiful. "It's just that I haven't seen another Rider's mark before."

"Well… now you know."

Eight

"Do you think I will be a good Dragon Rider?"

Sitting along the bank of the river, I gazed up at the stars. Aurora had her head down beside me, her tail slightly curved around my body. Markus had left not long ago after one of the king's men had called for him. The soldier said something about an issue at Noblemen Country, and the Riders needed to have a meeting.

I, on the other hand, wasn't allowed to go, since I hadn't been presented to the court yet. Markus had explained that each Rider is presented in front of the court in a grand ball, where the new Riders are shown off. Each Rider is presented with their own armour and uniform to wear. From there, they decide on their choice of weapon.

You will make a great Rider.

Moving her head to my lap, Aurora's eyes closed and a soft snort came from her nose.

We have a lot ahead of us.

I took a deep breath and shook my head. "I just feel like I'll be looked down upon. Everyone is expecting another male Rider. How am I meant to get them to see me just like them?"

Lifting her head, she gazed down at me, before moving her head up towards the sky, and releasing a loud roar.

Then we show them.

Releasing an excited squeal, I couldn't remove the smile plastered on my face even if I wanted to. She was right. It didn't matter if the other villagers didn't think I was capable of protecting them; I was going to show anyone who doubted me just what I could do.

Walking back towards the cabin, I noticed how everything seemed to be repaired. And in just a few hours I would be leaving. I wouldn't be able to come back to the village any more, nor would I be able to help my mother in the harvesting month. Knowing she would have to work just as hard to make the harvest month successful, I'd be lying if I told her it hadn't caused me to worry. I took one last deep breath and sighed.

"Abagail, there you are." Turning my head in the direction where the voice came from, I noticed the king with a few of his men.

Bowing my head in respect, I heard him chuckle. "There is no need to bow down to me. You are my Rider, after all."

"How can you accept me so easily, knowing I'm a girl and not a man?" I asked.

"I see your potential, Abagail." Moving closer towards me, the king placed his hand on my shoulder. With a gentle smile, he continued, "I believe the gods have reasons for what they do, and... who is a king to question a god?"

"I just hope I don't let your kingdom down, Your Majesty."

Squeezing my shoulder, he smiled down at me. "You won't."

Moving his hands from my shoulder, he turned to face the men behind him and clapped his hands. Upon his command, the two men walked towards us, carrying a large saddle, which appeared to be the very kind of saddle the Riders used. At the mere thought that it could be mine, a nervous smile crossed my face.

"Is this for Aurora?" I asked.

"Your dragon is female?" questioned the king, shocked.

Nodding my head, I frowned. "Why? Has there yet to be a female dragon, too?"

Shaking his head, I watched as a high priest stepped forward. "There hasn't been a female dragon in a long time." Turning towards the king, the priest lowered his voice. "Your Majesty, we could use this dragon to breed more eggs and…"

"Over my dead body!" I growled, cutting him off.

Stepping closer, I reached down to grab the small dagger strapped to my thigh as the sound of Aurora's scream echoed throughout the village. Flying up into the sky from the forest, Aurora spread her wings wide as she dived down to the ground.

Landing behind me, wings still out wide, she lowered her body, before roaring, showing her teeth as she did so. Pulling the dagger from its sheath, I held it out towards the priest. I knew that what I was doing would be classed as treason towards the high priest, but I didn't care at this moment.

The sound of running feet, followed by the sound of other dragon screams through the air, filled my ears.

"Abagail! Lower your dagger!" a voice yelled.

Quickly glancing at the voice, I noticed William and Markus reaching down to hold their swords. Lifting my head higher, I felt my vision once again intensify, colours heightening. I was tapping into Aurora.

Growling, Aurora turned towards the other dragons that had landed. Her tail swiped at the air in warning, before coming to rest near my side.

Backing away, the king held up his hands in a sign of peace. "Abagail, please lower your weapon," he whispered.

Lifting my head, I watched as the priest backed away. I knew my eyes had changed colour, since everyone was looking at me, or it could have been the fact I held a weapon, but right now I was too focused on this one old man to really care.

"You dare insinuate to the king you would use my dragon as a breeding vessel!" I spat.

"What?" William asked, looking around at the men that had gathered.

I gripped the dagger tighter in my hand. "This high priest wants to use my dragon as a breeding vessel for his own gain!"

Markus moved closer towards me. Reaching out, he wrapped his hand around my own which held the blade, and gently pushed it down. Moving to my side, he whispered in my ear. "We will not let him harm your dragon, Abagail."

Moving my gaze to his, I bit my bottom lip. *Stand down, Aurora*, I thought, as I looked back at the king. "If you harm my dragon or use her in any way, I will not hesitate to end you."

Frowning, but happy I was listening, the king nodded. "Your dragon will not be harmed. It was never my intention to use you or her."

Satisfied with his response, I placed the dagger back into the sheath. Looking up at the priest through my lashes, I noticed he was fearful in stance.

"How dare you insinuate using the Rider's dragon?" William growled, causing his dragon to do the same.

"You don't understand. Her dragon is a female; we could have made more eggs."

"And you think this was the way to do it?" he yelled.

Lowering his gaze to the floor, the priest shook his head. "No, Your Highness. I apologise for my actions. We just don't know where the sacred egg is."

I am the egg they speak of.

"What?" Turning around, I looked up at Aurora. Her gaze was on the priest.

"What is it?" asked the king.

Turning my head slightly, I looked at the king. "Aurora said *she* is the egg you speak of."

Chuckling to himself, the priest shook his head. "That's impossible."

While he waved his hand in dismissal at me, I turned to look at the other Riders. "The sacred egg had been around since the first founder dragons. There is no way that dragon is the egg from the cave."

Your dreams, Abagail. Tell them about how we first met.

"She's right." Looking back at the priest, I smirked. "She is the egg. I first met her in my dreams. She was in a cave surrounded by water. There was water falling constantly from the ceiling."

"The cave was hidden under a waterfall." The big fat man from this morning made his way to the front and looked at the king. Wiping his mouth, he said, "We had gone there once on a mission to seek answers. We had to swim under the falling water to get to the cave; even then there was still water falling from the rock walls."

Placing his hand under his chin, the king looked to be deep in thought. I knew what I was saying was the truth. Each Rider has these dreams, and we all swore by them to be real. Most of my dreams did take place at the cave. I couldn't help but think that maybe there was a reason for that.

"Even when I was awake, if I looked into the water, I'd see her eyes," I whispered.

The king turned to me and smiled. "I feel as if a meeting is in order," the king declared. "We should head back to the kingdom..." I watched as the king's eyes darkened slightly as he gazed at the forest. "We know not of who may be in these parts."

"Of course, Your Majesty." Bowing his head, the priest turned to his horse, not before eyeing me up and down. I looked away and lowered my gaze.

"Men, place the saddle onto Abagail's dragon. William, show her how to fasten it. She needs to learn."

"Of course, Father." Moving towards me, William gripped my forearm. Tugging me slightly towards him, he whispered, "You are really lucky my father hasn't sentenced you to death for your act."

I frowned and tried pulling my arm away in vain. "Well, if the High Priest didn't want to use my dragon as a breeding vessel, maybe I wouldn't have drawn my weapon."

He shook his head. "Your emotions are linked to your dragon. You drew your weapon not just because you were upset, but also because of your dragon's influence on you."

Gritting my teeth, I tried to pull away again, only to have him tighten his grip. Growling down at us, Aurora moved towards me.

Looking up at her, William smiled. "I will not hurt your Rider."

Snorting, Aurora tilted her head to the side. *Let's hope you don't, then. You're too handsome to eat.*

Catching the laugh that wished to be released, I looked up at William.

"What?" Frowning down at me, he tilted his head the same way Aurora had.

Gazing up at Aurora, I couldn't help the smile that graced my lips. "She just asks for you to show me how to use the saddle so we can leave."

Shaking his head, he released me. "Very well."

Laying on her stomach, Aurora allowed the soldiers to place the saddle over her back. "Can you please lift yourself a little?" William asked. Looking towards me, she did as she said.

How can a dragon say no to him? she chuckled.

Reaching under her, I watched as William pulled the thick leather strap around to a buckle. Moving closer to him, I could feel the heat coming from his body, almost wishing me to move closer. Shaking my head, I watched as he threaded the leather strap through a buckle, before pulling.

Aurora grunted in distaste at the restricting garment. Placing my hand on her side, I gave it a gentle tap, hoping to ease her discomfort.

"So I just put it through the buckle till it clips down?" He made it look so easy, and here I was still trying to get my head around all the little straps.

Nodding, William placed his hands together. "Hop up, Rider."

Smirking up at me, I watched as his playful demeanour made a welcome return. Laughing, I placed my hand on a small handle on top of the saddle. Placing my right foot in his hands, I gripped tighter to the handle.

"Okay, I'm going to give you a small boost. Make sure you swing your leg over, as if you were riding a horse."

Nodding my head, I did as I was told. Before I knew it, I was sitting on top of Aurora. Moving slightly to get more comfortable, I welcomed the feeling of being connected to Aurora again. I felt her energy flowing through me as I looked around at the other Riders. They too were getting onto their dragons.

Your mother is here, whispered Aurora. Turning her head to the left, she bowed her head.

Turning my head towards the farming area, I watched as Mother walked towards me, hands clasped together. Rushing to my side, she gently grabbed onto my ankle. "You make sure you eat all your meals, okay?"

"I will," I whispered.

Reaching into the pocket of her dirty waist-apron, she pulled out a necklace with a ring on it. Reaching up to grab my hand, she opened my palm, placing the object in my hand. "This was your father's ring."

"What?" I whispered.

Looking down at the object, I noticed a small engraving on the inside. "Robert, Samantha. Forever together," I whispered. Looking back down at Mother, I smiled through the tears that, up until now, I hadn't realised were forming in my eyes.

"Thank you." Tying the necklace around my neck, I took a deep breath. If I left right now, I wouldn't be able to look after her. I would be disappointing her.

You will never do such a thing. She is proud of you, Abagail.

Biting my bottom lip, I watched as Aurora gently nudged her head into my mother's side. Smiling, Mother gently patted her head. "You look after my baby girl."

With my life.

Moving her head away, she released a loud roar. Smiling, I felt pride surge through my veins. Gazing down at my mother, I tried my best to give a reassuring smile.

"I will be back to see you," I promised. And this was a promise I will keep.

"Let's ride!" yelled the king. Kicking his heel into his horse, he made his way down the path, followed by his guards and the priest.

"Let's fly, Riders!" William yelled.

The sound of dragons roaring in agreement filled my ears, before they took to the sky. Gripping tighter onto the saddle, I took one final look at my mother and the rest of the villagers.

"Stay safe," I yelled. Gazing down at Aurora, I couldn't help the smirk that formed on my lips. "Now let's show them just what we are made of."

With pleasure.

As Aurora released the loudest roar I had heard, I gripped tighter onto the saddle as she shot up into the air, chasing after the other Riders.

I could hear the happy cheers of the villagers, followed by my mother's yell: "I love you!"

Tightly closing my eyes, I took a deep breath. My new future was starting to begin, and I couldn't be more excited.

Nine

As we arrived at the castle grounds, King Albert was waiting for us. The Riders had decided to go on a little joyride around the kingdom, leading to Talios and William showing off their flying skills. Both were very talented in flying, with William even being able to move around his dragon whilst in mid-air. I had tried to attempt to move, but every time my hands came off the saddle, I felt like my insides were trying to come out.

Facing towards us, the king looked upwards as all the Riders landed in a big clearing, not too far from a massive stone shelter. I was shocked by the sheer beauty of the castle grounds. The grass was a different shade of green here. Along the small gravel paths, flaming torches were alight, with a few guards standing near them. I could only assume they were here because of the king, and not a regular guard post.

Jumping down from his dragon, William headed towards his father. Placing a hand over his chest, he bent his upper body slightly in a sign of respect. This was welcomed with a hearty clap on his back, before King Albert walked towards the rest of the Riders.

"See you all had a little fun on your way here!" laughed the king. A few of the Riders laughed and spoke about the ride amongst themselves, some even play-fighting a little.

As I got down from Aurora, my legs felt numb from the flight, causing me to trip. Before I could fall, hands shot out, grabbing me around my waist, holding me steady, before letting me go. Turning to see who had stopped my fall, I gazed up into Markus' bright blue eyes that shone with mischief. As he took a small step back, I realised he had a smug grin on his face.

"I thought you would've grown into your clumsy legs by now, Abagail," he said, a small chuckle escaping his lips.

Looking him over, I smiled playfully. "And here I thought you would've grown into your armour."

Laughing, he reached out and squeezed my shoulder. "How I've missed you, Abagail."

With a final glance at me, Markus moved to stand with the rest of the Riders. Looking up at Aurora, I watched as she tilted her head, nudging me towards the group.

Go and make us proud, my Rider.

Smiling up at her, I nodded. Standing next to a tall, stocky man with blond hair, I lifted my head high. I wasn't going to let these men intimidate me in any way. I was going to show them a female could be just as much a Rider as any man could.

Walking down the line of Riders, the king gazed at each one of us. "Today we helped a village rebuild," he said. His voice seemed to echo through the open field. "Today we also found our new Rider."

A few snorts followed, causing the king to frown. Turning towards one of the Riders, King Albert frowned down at him. "That is no way to treat a fellow Rider. She was picked just like all of you, and I demand respect be brought to her." Moving so he stood in front of the line, the king moved his gold cape away from his still-armoured body. It was only then that I realised he had a long sword holstered to his hip. I didn't think he would be armed, considering he was on his own land.

Resting his left hand over the top of his sword, he continued, "You will *all* help her settle in, and you will teach her the ways of the Riders. Understood?"

"Yes, Your Majesty," William said.

Nodding his head in approval, the king continued, "In a few days' time, Abagail will be going on her first patrol down to Noblemen Country. William, Markus and Matthew will accompany her."

Looking down the line to me, the king's demeanour became much more serious. "Noblemen Country is not something to take lightly. There are nothing but thieves and liars there, so I suggest you watch your back on your patrol. Understood?"

Bowing my head slightly, I nodded. "Yes, Your Majesty."

He waved his hand to one of the lady's maids; she bowed to the king and left, before coming back with a man. A tall gentleman wearing a fitted suit with a phoenix on his left breast pocket, stood beside the king. He had slicked-back grey hair, and a moustache covered the top of his lip, with the sides curled upwards.

"This gentleman here will be organising your outfit for the ball in two days' time."

Frowning, I looked around at the other Riders. "And what will happen in the ball?" I questioned.

Turning towards me, William quickly glanced at his father before speaking. "Each Rider is to go through an acceptance ball. It's a way of introducing yourself to the land and people of Athena."

Nodding my head, I looked at the ground. A ball was the last thing I wanted to go to. Everyone was expecting another male Rider, and I bet the ladies of the town were probably getting ready now as we spoke. I could only imagine the looks on their faces as I walked in. Horror, shock and, most of all, I could picture their questioning gazes on me.

"You will be spoken to further tomorrow when you are fitted for your gown. For now, I want everyone to head to their quarters for rest."

Standing tall, all the Riders bowed towards the king. Following their lead, I did the same.

Once the king left, Markus turned towards me. "I'll show you to your quarters." I looked back at Aurora, worried at where she would go. As if reading my thoughts, Markus added, "Tell her to follow the other dragons."

"You heard him," I whispered.

How could I not? Snorting air out through her nose, she turned around to follow the other dragons. *You stay safe.*

Walking into the castle, I couldn't help but gaze at all the paintings that lined the walls. All the fellow kings and queens were on the walls, including a painting of William standing next to a girl in a dark red floor-length gown. Before I was able to take a good look, Markus pulled me towards a small staircase that led up to another marble floor.

As we reached the top of the staircase, I noticed a long hallway littered with doors.

"This is where the Riders sleep," he said, gesturing to the long hallway. "We all have our own rooms." Reaching into his pocket, he pulled out a small gold key. "And we all have the key to our own rooms," he said, as he handed me the key and gave me a reassuring smile.

As he moved towards the furthest door to the left, I watched as he twisted the knob to open it up to a fairly large room. This room was easily the size of my hut back home.

The room itself was painted white. A window stood at the far end, with a small balcony that overlooked the River of Peace. I could see the cliff I used to sit at, dreaming about becoming a Dragon Rider. Smiling at the thought, I couldn't help but think how much things had changed so quickly.

"It will be your birthday soon," Markus said, catching me off-guard.

Turning around, I was met with his breathtaking smile. "I thought you'd forgotten."

Shaking his head, he went to take a step closer, but stopped when a female's voice entered the room. "Markus?" she whispered.

Standing behind Markus was a beautiful girl with light blonde hair. She wore a dark navy floor-length gown, and a small crown sat neatly on her head. Turning around and walking towards the girl, I watched in horror as Markus bent down to kiss her. At the sight in front of me, I felt my heart break. He had found a lover. Blinking away the tears that threatened to fall, I released a shaky breath. Biting my bottom lip, I dared to look at the girl. As if sensing my gaze, her smile faltered a little.

"Who are you?" She spoke with confidence and grace, and I immediately knew she was of the royal family.

Lifting my head high, I cleared my throat before speaking. "My name is Abagail Stone. I'm from the village of Knights Edge."

Nodding her head, she smiled. "Did you lose your home? Is that why you've been brought here?" she asked.

Chuckling, Markus grabbed her hand. Bringing it to his lips, he placed a gentle kiss on the top of her hand. Smiling down at her, he shook his head. "No, my love, she is the new Rider."

A shocked gasp escaped her lips. She frowned slightly, and I watched as she tried to look everywhere but at me. "I see." Pulling her hand away from Markus, she turned for the door. "It is late; get some rest, *Rider*." Emphasising my title, she turned slightly, gazing at me from the corner of her eyes, before leaving.

"That is the princess," Markus whispered. He seemed to be in awe of her, only causing my anger to grow.

Frowning, I looked at him. "Does the king know you are courting his daughter?" I couldn't help the anger that slowly seeped through my words. I was hurt. I had waited for the day to see Markus again, only to have my vision of a happy life with him ripped out right from my chest.

Frowning, he shook his head. "The king has had a word. His son isn't quite happy with the arrangement I have with the princess, but neither of us feel those opinions should come between us." With that, he turned and left the room.

Releasing the breath I was holding, I sank down on the bed. I had left everything behind willingly, knowing that I would have Markus here. Being gone for three years, of course, was a long time, but I guess I had hoped somewhere he had felt something more. I bit my bottom lip and swallowed the tight lump that had formed in my throat.

Sleep, for tomorrow is our day.

Aurora was right. Tomorrow will be the day I am presented to the land, and my time as a Dragon Rider is going to start. Kicking off my boots, I laid back on the bed. For the first time in a while, sleep had come easily to me.

Ten

The sound of banging entered my dreams, stirring me from my deep sleep. I didn't want to wake from my blissful dream of when Markus and I were kids. We were playing by a lake. He was chasing me around the lake as he splashed water in my direction. How I missed spending time with him like we did when we were kids.

Opening my eyes, I gazed up at the white roof, my thoughts going back to everything that had happened. I was now a Dragon Rider, living inside the kingdom and protecting the land. Although the thought of being a Dragon Rider still scared me, I knew the Founder Dragons wouldn't make a mistake with who they chose, and nor would the High Priest's book.

The sound of banging started once again, followed by a gentleman's voice. Moving the blanket from my legs, I headed towards the door. Grabbing a small navy blue robe from a chair situated near the door, I unlocked it to see the man that would be organising my ballgown standing there with a frown on his face. His suit today was of gold colour, the phoenix symbol still on his breast pocket.

Looking up at the man, I tightened the robe around me. "Can I help you?"

Pushing me aside, he walked into the room. "There is much to be done today." Turning to me, he clapped his hands, eyes roaming my form. "Yes, the gown will do just fine."

"The what?" I questioned.

"Your acceptance gown. I've been up all night making it for you." Clapping his hands twice, two young maids walked into my room, carrying a light blue gown. Gently placing the gown down on the bed, one of the young maids walked towards me.

Gripping my arm, she pulled me towards the small bathing room. "Please follow me, Rider." After pushing me into the hallway, and towards the bathing room, the young maid stood facing the door. "Please bathe. No need to dress; just wrap the towel around yourself."

Nodding my head, I turned towards the running water. The water was coming from the River of Peace, but had been heated by the maids. I had never seen a place like this before. The room almost looked like a cave, a giant circular pool situated in the middle of the room, before heading towards the edge of a balcony. Stepping into the water, I could feel all the tension drain away. It was almost as if the healers had used their magic. Laughing at the thought, I sank deeper into the water.

Closing my eyes, I felt my mind drift off.

You seem relaxed, Rider.

Shocked by the sudden voice that entered my mind, I jolted up in the water, causing some of it to spill over the sides.

"Is everything okay?" squeaked the young maid.

Turning towards the panicked maid, I nodded. "Yes," I whispered. Frowning, I gazed down at the water.

Do not be afraid of me, Abagail, for I am the High Priest.

"What?" I whispered. "But I thought the priest that came to collect me was..."

No, he was one of the many priests that go to the Riders, the voice explained. It was a mixture between a husky and sweet; almost as if the two were talking over each other. *I am unable to leave the grounds in fear of an attack, but we shall meet soon.*

The feeling of someone grabbing my shoulder snapped me out of my thoughts. Turning my head towards the person, I saw the young maid staring down at me. "Rider? You have been quiet for some time," she said.

Taking a deep breath, I nodded. "I'm sorry. I must still be tired."

Nodding, she held out the towel. "We must get you ready for your acceptance ball." I wrapped the towel around myself, making sure it wouldn't fall, as I lifted myself from the water. As we left the bathing room, the sound of voices had me grabbing the towel tighter. Looking towards the end of the hall, I saw that William and a guard had stopped and were now looking up at me.

Heat crept up my neck as I watched William's eyes look upon my body. Even though I had something covering myself, although it was a small amount of fabric, I couldn't help but feel I was exposed to the two men. Bowing to the prince, the young maid turned back to me. "Please follow me, Rider," she said once more. Moving my gaze from William's, I followed the maid back to my room.

"Good, you're back." Clapping his hands, I watched as the man whistled. "You will look stunning in your gown, I assure you. I can see it now." He gazed at me with a far-off look, as if he was already at the ball, watching his creation walk down to the hungry crowd below.

Turning to the man, the young maid bowed. "Sir Philip, may I be excused?" Dismissing the girl with his hand, Philip turned to the gown lying on my bed. When did he put that there?

"Change into this, Rider."

"My name is Abagail," I said.

I didn't like being called Rider. I had a name, and I wished for it to be used. Nodding his head, he waved his hands, dismissing me. "Of course, of course. Now change, Rider."

Gritting my teeth, I snatched the gown from the bed. Turning to Philip, I raised my brows at him. "Are you not going to leave?"

Rolling his eyes, he turned around. "You can change with me in the room," he said, as he fixed the jacket of his suit. With a shake of his head, he mumbled. "She would think I hadn't seen a woman's body before."

As quickly as I could, I put the gown on, careful to not let the towel fall. The fabric of the dress felt nice on my skin, and I was thankful that it wasn't made of an itchy material. The gown was light blue, with the leg area open just above my knee. Around my middle was a silver-plated armour piece. My left shoulder was exposed, showing my dragon mark, and I couldn't help the pride that flowed through my body at the sight of it. Even with the small amount of armour around my middle, I didn't find it restricting in the slightest.

Although it was slightly revealing the top of my chest, I couldn't help but become awestruck. It was like the old stories Mother used to tell me about, where the royal family would hold parties every month to celebrate the peace. But since the war, there hadn't been one.

"You look stunning, does she not, my Prince?" At the mention of the prince, I spun around towards Philip.

Standing beside him was Prince William. He was dressed in his own formal wear. His tuxedo was white with gold trimming, the phoenix symbol on his breast pocket. Strapped to his waist was a sword with a gold handle.

"She looks breathtaking," he whispered.

Once again, I watched as his eyes roamed my body, but this time I didn't let him.

"Your eyes shouldn't wander around, my prince." Using his title in front of people was in my best interest. I didn't want to be accused of disrespecting the royal family.

Chuckling to himself, the prince bowed slightly. "My apologies, my lady, for the rude gesture on my behalf. I will train my eyes to stay above."

At his words, I felt myself smile. He was having fun with his little act, and for some reason unknown to me I joined in. "Your eyes were not made for wandering a lady's body that does not belong to you, my prince."

Smirking, I watched his eyes dance with humour. Bowing once again to me, he held his arm out towards the door. "Then will the fair lady take my peace offering and allow me to take her to her dragon?"

Bowing my head in agreement, I turned to Philip. "The gown is beautiful, Sir Philip." After bowing my head to him in respect, I moved towards William. As he crooked his elbow, I gently placed my hand in through it.

Making our way out of the castle towards the clearing we had landed in yesterday, I gazed out at the scenery. Guards were walking around the field as they went about their patrols. A few servants were carrying items towards the middle of the field. Chairs and small tables were already placed around the field, with a small podium where the king would sit. Turning towards William, I frowned. "Is the acceptance ball in the field?"

Nodding, he held his hand out towards a few dragons that lay in the morning sun. I'd never seen these dragons before, and I couldn't help but wonder where their Riders were.

"Those dragons are too big to fit into the hall, so we move the celebrations outside, where they have their own way of welcome," he said, gesturing to the vast field.

"What do the other dragons do?" I was curious. I hadn't heard any stories of their own acceptance ritual before.

Placing his free hand over my own, he gave it a gentle squeeze. "It's not my right to say." Before I could question him, someone called my name.

Looking to my left, I noticed Markus and the princess walking towards us. Markus was dressed in a dark green suit. His shoulders held silver-plated armour that reminded me of dragon's scales. Beside him, the princess wore a ruby red floor-length gown, her long blonde hair cascading down her back and chest. As she noticed me, she scowled my way, clearly unhappy at my presence.

Taking a deep breath, I lifted my head slightly. In some way, I hoped it would make me look unaffected by their status. Looking towards William, Markus bowed. "Your Highness."

Clenching his jaw, William nodded. "I see you're with my sister."

Nodding, Markus smiled down at the princess. "Yes, Princess Anna was keeping me company."

Smiling, Anna turned towards her brother, but her smile fell when she noticed my gaze on her. "So I wasn't dreaming when you said you were a Rider," she whispered.

Stepping forward, she assessed me. "How can you protect me if something happens?" Confused by her words, I looked at Markus and William. They too had frowns on their faces.

Looking at Anna, I took a deep breath. "I mean no disrespect to you, princess, but I'm sure there are plenty of men here willing to come to your aid."

Anger crossed her face as she lifted her head. It almost seemed like she wanted me to drop to my knees and grovel. Sadly for her, I wasn't the type to do that.

Her once calm eyes seemed to burn with something more. Walking closer to me, she touched the fabric of my gown. "These silks seem too good for someone like you."

Glaring down at her, I felt Aurora's power surging through me. Frowning, Anna took a step back. "You dare connect to your dragon in front of me?" she hissed.

Walking in front of me, William placed his hand on his sister's shoulder. "I'm sure her dragon was contacting her." Turning to me, he smiled. "Am I wrong?"

Shaking my head, I looked at Anna. "I'm sorry, princess, but the prince is correct. My dragon was asking where I was."

Snorting, the princess sighed. "Aren't the dragons meant to be under your control, not the other way around?"

"I am nothing but equal to my dragon, princess." Biting my bottom lip to stop Aurora's power, I blinked a few times. I could still feel Aurora's anger flowing through me as the sound of heavy steps hitting the earth echoed through the clearing.

Standing behind Markus and Anna, Aurora glared down at the two.

Just say the word, and I'll finish them.

Shaking my head, I looked up at Aurora. *Just give them a little fright.*

With pleasure.

Standing on her hind legs, Aurora spread her wings out wide And released a loud roar from her throat. Anna jumped, startled by the sudden sound. Looking up at Aurora, the princess blinked. "What is this dragon doing disrespecting its princess? All dragons are the same. They don't care for their royals!"

"It's a female dragon," William said. A small smirk played on his lips, as if he was finding this interaction funny.

Moving to stand beside Aurora, William gently touched the side of her neck, not too far from her mark. "This dragon is female, sister."

Stepping closer to Aurora, Anna looked her over. "That's impossible."

Don't insult me, Aurora hissed.

Smiling, I moved to her side. The saddle that had been placed on her back last night had been replaced with a silver armour saddle, the sides a light gold; and as she moved, it was almost like millions of little stars were shining right in front of me.

Bringing her head down to me, she gently touched my stomach with her nose, causing my mark to tingle.

You look like a true Rider.

Rubbing the bridge of her nose, I smiled. "Thank you." Placing my arm around her neck as if to hug her, I lowered my voice so only she could hear. "Don't do anything that would get yourself in danger."

Then let's pray to the High Priest she stays quiet.

"What are you saying to your dragon, Rider?" Walking towards me, Anna gripped my arm. Glaring down at her arm, I pulled away from her grip, causing her to stumble slightly. I didn't like being touched. It was something Alex knew about all too well. Before I was able to answer, someone had cut me off.

"A conversation with one's dragon is sacred," William said. "It's not for you to know their words, Anna."

"Well, then..." Placing her hands back on Markus' arm, she smiled up at him, before turning her gaze back to me. Her gaze held something I couldn't quite figure out. It almost seemed as if she was waiting for me to slip up.

Smirking at me one last time, she turned to her brother. "Let's hope she knows how to protect herself, then."

William stiffened beside me at her words. I didn't understand what she meant. Protect herself? Why would I need to protect myself?

Dragons fight to see where they stand, and so do you. Snapping my head towards Aurora, I watched as she lowered her head in apology to me. *I must fight to be accepted as a dragon.*

Eleven

"I can't do this," I whispered to the young maid.

I had been pacing behind the doors for what felt like hours now, trying to find a way to escape. I wasn't ready to be announced to the Land of Athena. I knew they would be disappointed in me once they saw me. Women from across the land had made their way here in high hopes of impressing the new male Rider; but sadly for them, this time they were dressing up for a woman.

Taking a deep breath, I peeked through the cream-coloured curtains that showed the vast field. It was full of tables and chairs, all adorned with white flowers. Gold ribbons were tied around the chairs, with the phoenix symbol situated on the back. Sitting at the far end of the field, King Albert, Prince William, and Princess Anna sat on their thrones. They all looked so royal in their formal outfits. William wore his white suit with pieces of armour on his shoulders and chest. His hair was slicked back, which made his blue eyes shine under the light of the moon. Anna wore her floor-length ruby red gown with her hair pulled into a high bun, while King Albert wore a white tuxedo with gold trimming.

Taking a deep breath, I moved away from the window. I sighed as I turned to face the young maid. "How long till the acceptance ball starts?"

Looking towards one of the guards at the door, she nodded. Turning around, the guard opened the door slightly to exchange a few words with the announcer, before returning to us.

"We shall begin now."

Biting my bottom lip, I clenched my shaking hands together. Was I really ready to announce myself as the Rider? I couldn't help but feel that I'd be letting so many people down by showing myself.

Before I was able to make a run for it, I heard the announcer's voice. "Ladies and gentlemen, today we gather to welcome the new Dragon Rider to our lands." The crowd came to life with applause and cheers, causing my nerves to spike. I felt like my stomach was in my throat, and the foul taste of bile almost had me running from the scene.

Moving me towards the door, the young maid looked over my attire. Once satisfied I was ready, she moved towards the far side of the wall. Taking a deep breath, I readied myself.

"I would like to announce to you all, in front of the king," spoke the announcer. His voice echoed through the closed oak doors, only adding to my shaking nerves. Moving his hand towards the king, he bowed his head. "The new Dragon Rider, from the village of Knights Edge!"

The doors opened, revealing the crowd. Now being able to see everything, I was shocked at how many people were actually here. Those who couldn't have a seat stood around the outer tables. There had to be at least a thousand people here, all talking and dancing.

The crowd fell silent. Whatever life was there only a few moments ago had seemingly vanished. After checking I was still breathing, I looked out into the crowd to see those attending the event. So many faces were staring right back at me; some were wide-eyed in shock and others in what surprisingly appeared to be joy. In all the time I spent worrying about how people would react, never did it cross my mind that anyone would be pleased.

Taking a deep breath at the edge of the steps, I closed my eyes. I was ready. I needed to take my place and make my father proud of me.

Let us be known and show our enemies who we are.

"Please welcome your new Rider, Abagail Stone!"

Aurora let out a loud roar just as the announcer yelled my name. Taking a step forward into the light, I watched as a few people in the crowd started to clap and murmur amongst themselves. The sound of another roar echoed throughout the field as Aurora flew over the top of us. As I watched her circle back around, I moved down the steps to where a few guards were standing.

Walking further onto the field, I stopped at a clearing, with the crowd right in front of me. It was set up for those who wished to dance, and I knew it would also be used for when Aurora had to fight later that night.

Landing behind me on all fours, Aurora held her head up high.

Let us have our moment.

"Yes," I whispered.

I began to smile as I walked towards the middle of the field, just in front of where the king was seated. Bowing my head to him in respect, my ears caught onto a few whispers from the crowd, now wild with questions and speculation.

"How?"

"It doesn't make sense."

"This can't be real. She must have used dark magic on that dragon."

Aurora let out a threatening growl at the comment. Moving behind me, she lowered her head and growled in warning. Rising to his feet, King Albert looked over his people.

"Today we welcome the very first female Rider and dragon."

Gasps echoed throughout the field. They had thought Aurora was another male dragon. "But, Your Majesty, there hasn't been a female dragon for centuries," one of the Council members bleated. He wore a black tuxedo and by the looks of his off-coloured hair, he was wearing a wig.

The king's face hardened into a stern scowl of contentment. His hand rose to bring silence among the crowd. The king looked over his people. "Regardless of what your thoughts are, Abagail was chosen just like the rest of the men here before you. She has not used such magic from the Dark Mountains, and I have witnessed their bond first hand."

"I, too, have seen the way they act," William said, as he stood. Placing his hand on the handle of the sword strapped to his waist, his eyes locked with mine. A strange tingle ran down my spine as his eyes danced with something unknown. "I have even had the honour of fighting beside Rider Abagail."

Smiling up at William, I gave a subtle nod. Winking at me, he turned and spoke to his father.

"The king was there the day we came for Abagail and witnessed her dragon protecting not only her but also Abagail's mother. They have a true bond, just like I have with mine. Do not question the High Priest... she knows the truth."

Bowing their heads in respect to the royal family, a few people looked my way. I could see how scared they were and they had a right to be. Never had a female Rider been picked, nor had there been a female dragon for far longer than any of their lifetimes.

King Albert smiled down at me, before looking back at his people. "Let us welcome our new Rider!" he shouted out to the crowd.

Cheers rang through the air as screams and claps followed.

"Let us commence the ritual."

"What?" I whispered in shock.

William mouthed an apology to me. Before I was able to react, I was pushed to the floor, landing with a loud thud. As I groaned in pain, Aurora roared, before jumping in front of me. Her tail curled around my body, working as a shield.

Getting to my feet, I looked around at my surroundings. A few of the other Riders had their weapons drawn. I didn't understand. Why was this happening?

They are testing us!

Aurora growled as she flashed her teeth at the Riders. Growling at the men, she went to take a step, but was hit from the side by another dragon. All I had been able to see was a flash of silver before she had been hit.

She was quick to flip herself upright, before extending her talons and skidding to a hasty stop. Stalking towards her, three dragons, all of a smaller height to Aurora, growled up at her. One of the dragon's scales were of sand-like colour; the other two seemed to be slightly off shades of brown, with one having a white tinge to it. Aurora growled at the three dragons that now circled her, and I watched in shock as one of them bit into her tail, causing her to scream in pain.

The people around us cheered at the dragons that were hurting Aurora. This wasn't right; how could they do this to one of their own. My breath quickened as pain shot through my stomach. Looking down, I bit my lip. I was feeling her pain. The legends I had read about in scrolls were true. A Rider could feel the pain of their dragon.

Clenching my teeth, I looked at the men in front of me with their weapons drawn. This wasn't a fair fight. I didn't have anything to help me. Looking around the field, I found a few soldiers watching the dragons fight. I knew I had no other choice.

"Shit!" I hissed.

Rushing towards one of the soldiers, I ripped his weapon from his scabbard. A shocked gasp left his lips as he turned around with a frown. Using the butt of the handle, I smacked it into the side of his head, knocking him unconscious. Turning around, I faced the other Riders, while I held my sword out in warning. Sickening smiles danced across their faces as they stalked closer to me. Flickering my gaze to Aurora, I noticed she was now being circled. Her claws were extended, with her teeth gleaming out at them.

Anger consumed me as I tapped into Aurora's strength. This was the first time we would be fighting together as one, and I was frightened. I wasn't sure what to do, but as her energy ran through me, I felt my nerves calming.

"Aurora!" I yelled. "Fly high!"

Releasing a loud scream, she shot up into the sky, followed by two of the dragons.

"Fight them with your size, Aurora! You're stronger than them!" I shouted.

With pleasure! Roaring in anger, she flew higher up into the night sky, narrowly missing the claws of a red dragon. Swooping to the side, she flung her tail into the side of the dragon's head, causing it to sway slightly in the air.

Looking back at the Riders that were now around me, I could see the looks in their eyes that screamed at me with joy. They were enjoying this. They were happy they were able to fight me, even though I was one of them. Lost in my thoughts, I hadn't noticed one of the Riders swinging his sword, until a stinging sensation hit my arm. Hissing in pain, I turned to see a cut on my upper arm, blood slowly seeping out of the open wound.

Gritting my teeth, I caught movement to my right. Lifting the sword, it clashed with a black sword, a loud ting sound echoing in my ears. Following along the sharp edges of the blade to its owner, I noticed it was the same small tubby man with the strange accent.

I gritted my teeth as I tried to push his weapon away, but failed. He was stronger than me, even when I was tapping into Aurora.

Pulling my sword away from his, I heard the crowd cheer as the dragons continued their fighting up above us. I'm screwed. I didn't know how to use a sword. Without my bow I was useless. I had never used a sword before, and the object in my hands felt foreign and heavy. I looked around frantically. No one had a bow. I was stuck with a weapon I had no idea how to use.

Biting my bottom lip, I knew there was no other choice. "Aurora!" I yelled. Finding an opportunity, I punched one of the men in the side of the face, causing him to stagger backwards, creating a gap in the circle.

Pushing my way through, I ran towards the edge of the cliff. I had no other choice. As if sensing what I was about to do, William stood from his chair, along with the king.

"Aurora, catch me," I whispered, before I reached the edge.

Moving to the side to avoid the talons of a dark grey dragon, Aurora flew higher into the sky, before closing her wings around herself and plummeting to the ground at full speed.

Don't let me fall, I thought.

Let's show them what we're made of, Aurora screamed once more as she flew closer and closer towards the ground.

"Now!" Rushing closer towards the cliff, I took a deep breath, before jumping over the edge.

"Abagail!" Markus screamed. William jumped down from the stage and rushed towards the cliff, just as Aurora passed the edge.

"Medics, guards, here now!" he yelled.

People stood from their chairs as they waited for their prince to announce the new Rider dead. But before he was able to reach the edge of the cliff, Aurora shot up into their line of view. Moving herself, so she was high in the air, she released a warning growl to the other Riders once more, before turning herself slightly.

"Unbelievable...!" King Albert whispered. "She caught her."

Looking down at the Riders with new-found vision, I clenched my fist. "Let's end this!"

Twelve

Gazing down below, I watched as the Riders scrambled beneath me. This had to end. I wasn't going to let them hurt me any longer. I had to show them I was capable of being a Rider just like them. Tapping into Aurora's sight, I roamed over the people, before catching sight of someone I didn't expect to see. Gazing up at me with hands clasped together tightly, my mother was muttering words. I couldn't make out what she was saying, but the look in her eyes was enough to snap me back into reality.

Moving my attention back to the Riders, I noticed a few had climbed onto their dragons. Clenching my fists, I thought of a plan. I could try and overthrow them, or I could trap them. "That's it!" I whispered.

"Aurora, cut them off!" I yelled.

Aurora dived down towards the Riders as she let out a bloodcurdling roar. Gripping onto her scales, I blinked away the stinging pain of the wind hitting my eyes. As we got closer to the ground, the sound of the crowd's cheers filled my ears.

"Abagail, you can do this!" I recognised the voice. It was William. He was cheering me on from the edge of the cliff, his dragon by his side.

You can do this, Rider, his dragon, Zor, whispered in my head.

"I can do this," I whispered.

As the ground became closer, my grip around Aurora tightened. "Now!" Releasing a loud growl, she opened her mouth as blue flames shot out, circling the Riders and the dragons, effectively cutting them off. Circling back around, she continued her action, closing in the circle. They were trapped. The dragons didn't have enough room to spread their wings to fly, and the Riders had no way of getting out.

Cheers rang through the air as the king stood from his throne; and, judging by the look on his face, he appeared pleased by the display. Landing on the ground, Aurora spread her wings wide in warning as a few guards hastily moved towards us.

Holding up his hand, the king yelled, "Leave them." On the king's demand, they moved back, still gripping their weapons in their hands.

Jumping down from Aurora, I gazed at the fire in front of me. Through the flames, I could see the other Riders and their dragons trying frantically to get out of the circle of flames. A few of the Riders had smiles on their faces, as if they were pleased with what I had done.

As I continued to gaze at the flames, I felt my mind start to wander. I suddenly felt like I wasn't in control of my own body, as I started walking towards the flames. It was as if someone was commanding me to put myself into the burning flames that would have me screaming in pain. But as I got closer to the flames, they moved aside, making an opening for me to walk through. Shocked gasps filled the air, as a few of the guards rushed towards me.

"She's using dark magic!" a villager screamed.

"Silence! There is no magic being used," yelled the king.

Stepping down from the platform, he walked towards me. The crowds stopped their chatter, as the king moved forward. Holding my hand up in front of me as if to touch the flames, I tilted my head. "Match over," I whispered. Throwing my hand to the side, the flames vanished. The only evidence of the fire was the burnt grass below.

The crowd cheered as their Riders were now defeated, and the horn sounded for their defeat. I had won. I was able to trap them and show my willingness to defend not only myself but my dragon, too. The feeling of being in control of my own body returned, causing me to stagger back slightly. My vision cleared and I began to regain composure.

Turning my head towards the sound of running feet, I was met with a hug from Alex. I placed my arms around him and laughed.

"You did it!" he cheered. Tightening my arms around him, I held him closer. Finally, I was a *Dragon Rider*. I could wear my mark with pride now and not hide it in fear of being discovered. Pulling back, I gazed at Alex, before I caught someone standing behind him.

"Mother," I whispered.

At the mere sight of her, I felt my walls falling. All the stress I had felt from the morning till now seemed to break me. Tears flooded my vision as I pulled away from Alex and jumped into the waiting arms of my dearest mother. As she kissed the side of my head, I felt her arms wrap around me.

"I am so proud of you, Abagail."

Nodding my head, I cried into her shoulder.

"Well done, Rider," Rider Talios said, causing me to pull away from my mother. Turning my head, I watched as he bowed slightly at me. Now that I could look at him, I noticed that, although he was short and tubby, his suit was made to his height. Smiling down at him, I nodded back in mutual respect.

"Thank you, Rider Talios."

Bowing his head once more, he moved back towards the eating area.

"Well done, Abagail," Mother whispered. "Your father would be so proud of you." At the mention of my father, I felt my body instantly relax. She was right. My father had always wanted me to follow my gut instinct, and tonight I did just that. Looking up at the night sky, I smiled. If he was looking down at me, I knew he would be proud.

Later that night, the festivities were in full swing. Music blasted into the air as people from across the land danced and mingled with other villagers. As I sat at my table, watching my mother trying to dance with Alex, I couldn't help the chuckle that left my lips as she stepped on his foot for the tenth time. I had warned Alex she couldn't dance, but he insisted that she dance with him. I could see by the look on his face he was regretting it now.

"Are you enjoying yourself, Rider?"

I turned towards the voice as William pulled out the seat next to me. "May I?"

Nodding, I smiled. "Of course, Your Highness."

With a small bow of his head, he sat down. Moving my gaze back to Alex and my mother, the smile returned almost instantly as yet again Mother stood on his foot.

"Your mother is quite the dancer."

Turning to William, I frowned. "Did you suddenly lose your ability to see?"

"I was merely stating that your mother isn't a bad dancer. That's if, of course, you ignore all the times she has probably stepped on that poor boy's feet."

Wincing as he watched other dance, I laughed. "She was never one to dance."

"And you?"

Looking down at the ground, I thought back to a happier time. Grabbing the ring tied around my neck, a small smile spread across my face. "Me and my father used to dance around the field. He'd get me to stand on his feet as he moved us across the grass in the summer time."

Leaning closer, William whispered, "He sounds like a great man."

"Was," I said. "Was a great man." Gazing up at William, I could see the curiosity in his eyes. He was eager to hear me continue. I took a deep breath and exhaled.

"He vanished when I was young. He was going hunting, but when it was time for him to come home, he didn't." Turning around, I watched as Mother laughed at all the festivities.

"I remember waiting for him outside our hut. When the sun had left the sky, Mother became worried and alerted the other hunters. After a while, they returned with his bow and arrows."

"They didn't find him?" he asked.

Shaking my head, I looked back to him. "They searched for days, but couldn't find any trace of his body."

Placing a hand on my shoulder, he gave it a gentle squeeze. His skin felt smooth on my bare skin, and I couldn't help the little shiver that ran down my spine. "I'm so sorry, Abagail. I can't imagine how you feel."

Shrugging, I smiled at him to mask my grief. "It's been a long time. It's okay."

But was it really? Was I really okay with not having him around? I wondered every day how my life might have been if he hadn't disappeared. Would he be here now to dance with my mother and would he be the reason for her laughter? Could I have had a sibling to share this world with?

Looking back at Mother and Alex, I felt pain in my chest. Mother worked so hard to make sure we had food on the table, and often kept working even when the ladies had left the field, in order to have coins for us to buy food and clothes. But now she wouldn't have to work as hard. I'd be able to provide for her.

Thirteen

"All right, everyone, gather round, please."

Smiling up at Markus, I followed him towards our trainer. It was two days after the ceremony, and it was now that my training would start. I had been woken by Markus' annoying voice before dawn with the news of my first training session.

I was informed that I'd have to be trained before I was even allowed on my first patrol. The patrols were usually harmless, but a few times Riders had been injured. Not everyone is fond of the Dragon Riders.

Standing beside Markus and Rider Talios, I looked down the line of men. To say I was nervous was an understatement. I had stayed awake for hours, talking to Aurora about all the possible things that would happen to me today. My greatest fear was to be denied the chance to go on a patrol. I wanted to show the other men that I was able to be a great Rider, just like them.

Taking a deep breath, I gazed at the older man in front of me. He seemed to be in his late forties. He had a strong jawline with a light shade of black stubble masking his tan skin. His eyes seemed to be an almost grey-like colour.

"Good morning, Riders. I see we have a new person here," he said.

Snorting, Talios shook his head. "This lass shouldn't even be here, if you ask me."

Turning to Talios, he smiled down at him. "Good thing I'm not asking you, then." Smirking, the man moved in front of me. Holding out his hand, he said, "My name is Sir Alaric Smith. You can just call me Alaric."

Shaking his hand, I smiled. "It's nice to meet you. My name is…"

"Abagail Stone," he said, cutting me off. Stepping back, he looked at the men. "It's hard not to know your name. You're the first female Rider, with a female dragon." Gazing back at me, he smirked. "Just because you're a lady doesn't mean I'm going to go easy on you." Tilting his head, his features hardened. "Do I make myself clear?"

"Yes, Sir Alaric."

Nodding, he smiled. "Good." Walking down the line, he gestured out to the empty field. "For those of you that have been through this training many times, you're in luck." Stopping, he turned to a man with shoulder-length black hair. "You don't have to practise today. In fact…" Moving his gaze down the line to me, he smirked. "You'll be helping me in grading Miss Stone in her training today. But I do still want you all to help her." A few groans followed, as one of the Riders glared down at me. Biting my bottom lip, I tried to focus on Alaric.

Moving to a rack of wooden swords, he threw one of them at one of the men. "We'll be teaching Abagail how to defend herself when the Dark King decides he wants to end her life."

A few claps echoed through my ears as some of the Riders moved towards the rack of swords. They seemed way too eager to help me, and I knew that there was no way they were even going to do that. I could tell they were going to try and humiliate me in front of everyone.

Taking a deep breath, I headed towards the sword rack. Grabbing one of the wooden swords, I made my way back to the line. Tightening my grip on the sword, I took a deep breath to calm my beating heart.

You can do this, Abagail.

Closing my eyes, I clenched my teeth. *But what if I can't?* I thought.

You are capable of a lot of things, Abagail. You just need to believe.

The feeling of something smacking the top of my head had me snapping out of my thoughts. "Now is not the time to be talking to your dragon, Rider."

Opening my mouth to speak, I stopped. I didn't know how he knew. Gazing up at Alaric, I frowned. "But how did…?"

"I know?" he asked.

Nodding my head, I waited for his reply. His face seemed to shift emotions as he gazed off into the distance. Sighing, Alaric cleared his throat. "That is a discussion for another day. For now, I want you to spar with someone."

Holding his hand out to one of the Riders, he smirked, "Rider Matthew, why don't you spar with Abagail?" Nodding his head, he walked towards me, weapon in hand, ready to start training.

I'm going to die, aren't I, Aurora?

Those are only wooden swords, she chuckled.

Yeah, swords that will hurt, I thought.

Well, don't get hit by them.

As if she had jinxed me, Matthew swung his sword, hitting me on the side of my ribs. Groaning in pain, I hissed through my teeth, "Easier said than done."

"Focus," Matthew whispered, just loud enough for me to catch. Since I had arrived, he had always been quiet. In the ceremony, he chose not to take part in my fighting, instead deciding to just stand by his dragon and watch. He intrigued me. His facial expression never seemed to change as he continued hitting me with the wooden sword.

Grabbing the side of my head that the sword had hit, I groaned. "Why couldn't I use a bow?"

Sighing, Matthew moved forward.

The sight of his hand coming closer to my face had me covering my head, waiting for the pain to hit, but it never came. Moving my arms, I saw Matthew was gazing down at me, his eyebrows raised.

"You're gripping it wrong," he stated.

Bending down to pick up the sword I dropped, he grabbed my wrist. Placing my hand over the base of the sword, he wrapped his hands over mine to grip the base. "You need to have a firm grip so you don't drop the sword."

Moving to my side, he guided me as he swiped at the air. It all seemed easy when he was helping me, but when he let go, it was as if I had learnt nothing.

Sighing, I dropped the sword. "I can't do this."

Bending down, he picked up the sword. "You can. It just takes time."

"I don't have time. The next patrol is in three days' time. I need to go on that patrol." I was getting angry. I wanted to go on that patrol, even if it meant spending all night out here. All the Riders wore their swords proudly, and here I am, unable to even swing one without hurting myself. Gritting my teeth in anger, I looked around the field. Off to the side were a few archery guards shooting arrows into the targets further down the field.

Smiling, I marched towards one of the bows on the ground. "Abagail, get back here now!" yelled Alaric. "Abagail!"

Ignoring his orders, I aligned an arrow with the bow and aimed at the target. Releasing my finger, I watched as the arrow flew through the air, before hitting the target with a loud thud.

"Well, I'll be damned," whispered Talios. "The lass can shoot a bow."

"She is a great archer."

Smiling at the familiar voice, I turned my head. "Good to see you remember my aim, Markus."

With a shake of his head, Markus chuckled. "How can one forget the day you shot at a tree, only missing my ear by a finger width."

Shrugging, I turned to Alaric. He looked angry. His face seemed a little red, and a frown had settled onto his face. Closing his eyes, he took a deep breath. "You disobeyed my orders."

"I'm sorry, it's just that…"

As he silenced me with his hand, I lowered my head.

"You disobeyed my orders... but I'm happy you did." Placing his hand on my shoulder, he gave it a gentle squeeze.

Lifting my gaze to meet his, I licked my chapped lips. "But I don't understand."

"You showed me you were capable of using a weapon. Even if that did mean you went against my orders." With a final pat on my shoulder, he turned to the rest of the men. "All right, let's all practice our flying!"

"Finally," Talios grinned. "Something Lye and I are good at." Walking towards his dragon, he gave it a slap on its front leg. Shaking his head, Lye turned to look at me. I watched as the dragon nodded its head and began to walk away from us, Talios sitting on its back.

Nudging the side of my body, Aurora moved in front of me. *Are you ready, Abagail?*

"You won't let me fall, will you?"

Snorting through her nose, she spread her wings wide. *Never.*

Once I was on her back, I grabbed hold of the saddle. Flying was the perfect chance for us to connect our sight and become one. Alaric had informed me that by being connected to your dragon could not only help save your life but also theirs. Both parties would be able to take energy if it was needed to survive or to fight. Knowing that Aurora and I would be able to protect each other settled my nerves.

Tightening my grip on the saddle, I looked around. Beside me, William was seated atop his silver dragon Zor. Zor's frame was big, but when standing beside Aurora, he looked tiny. "You ready to fly?" William asked.

Licking my chapped lips, I tilted my head. "I think so."

"Are you worried?" asked William.

"A little."

"There's no need to be. You and Aurora have flown before. Just take a deep breath and trust your dragon." Kicking his heel into the side of Zor, he moved closer towards us. "She is a strong dragon. She'll be able to help you."

I think I'm beginning to like this prince, Aurora chuckled.

Shaking my head, I looked towards the clearing. A few of the Riders were already flying up to the sky, with two of the dragons play-fighting. Smiling, I nodded my head. "All right, let's try this, shall we, Aurora?" As she gazed up at me, I watched her features soften.

Let's just take it easy for today.

"All right." Moving away from Zor and William, Aurora spread out her long wings. Flexing them a few times, she bent her lower body closer to the ground.

Hold on.

"What do you...?" Before I was able to finish, Aurora shot up into the sky, causing a little scream to be released from my throat. Tightening my grip on the saddle, I pulled my body closer to her own, almost causing me to lay on her. The feeling of wind stinging my skin and eyes had me shaking my head. It hurt. There was no denying that. Being dressed in a loose white t-shirt and brown leather trousers probably wasn't the best idea.

"Open your eyes, Abagail!" shouted William.

Opening my eyes, I was shocked by the view. We were way up in the sky. The castle almost looked like a small child's toy from up here. Laughing, I turned my head. Beside me, William and Zor flew at a slower pace, enjoying the nice clear weather and the warm sun.

"Try and connect with Aurora!" shouted William.

Biting, my lip, I frowned. "How?" I whispered.

Focus on my energy, Abagail. Will your vision to change.

Taking a deep breath, I exhaled slowly. The feeling of new energy flowed through my body, leaving small tingles in its wake. Closing my eyes, I waited till the feeling reached me, and once it did, I couldn't help the small sigh that fell from my lips. It almost felt like my body had been wrapped in the finest silk. Opening my eyes, everything around me was enhanced. The colours around me seemed brighter, and as I gazed at the ground below, I found my vision zooming closer to the ground.

"Woah!" I exhaled. I was thrilled.

Now you see what I see.

Moving my vision to the grand door of the castle, I spotted someone standing there in a long silver gown. *Anna.* "I thought she had a meeting this morning." Moving my vision closer to Anna, I noticed her mouth moving, her eyes fixated on me. Hissing in pain, I felt my eyes start to burn. "What's happening?" I groaned.

Aurora growled and moved towards the ground. *I don't know. I can't see.*

"Abagail!" a voice shouted. My eyes felt as if they were on fire, and by the sound of Aurora's pained scream, she, too, felt the same.

"Abagail, jump!" William shouted.

I grabbed hold of my shaking head. "It hurts," I hissed.

"You need to jump, now!" His voice sounded closer as the wind seemed to slowly drown out his words. Gritting my teeth, I let go of the saddle, and as Aurora turned her body, I fell to the side. The feeling of falling had me gasping for air, before the impact of the ground hit me hard on my side. Rolling over the hard ground, I groaned in pain as the sound of Aurora landing metres away from me filled my ears.

The side of my body burned and ached, but the pain in my eyes seemed far worse. Falling to my back, I gripped at my head and screamed.

The feeling of someone pulling my hands away from my head had me grunting in frustration. "Open your eyes," he whispered. Opening them, I was met with the blurred face of William. His blue eyes were now silver, his hair tousled from the flight.

Gripping my upper arm, he pulled me into a sitting position. "What happened?"

Looking to where I heard Aurora fall, I saw that she, too, was getting up, shaking her head to rid herself of the pain. I looked back at William, confused as ever. "I don't know."

Fourteen

Hissing in pain as the alcohol hit my skin, I gritted my teeth to stop myself from yelling in pain. After my little fall in training, Alaric had sent me straight to the healer, against my wishes. The last thing I wanted to do was see this woman who believed she could heal people; but when Alaric gave me a stern look, I had no other choice. Twitching as the damp cloth laced in alcohol hit my skin, I craned my neck in some way to calm my beating heart.

"Sit still," chided the healer.

The healer was an elderly lady with long grey hair. On her forehead was a symbol, one I had seen before that was used to ward off any evil spirits. She was dressed in a white gown that reached down to the floor, where it bunched up around her feet.

Rolling my eyes at the healer, I sighed. I wanted out of this room. It smelled like herbs and medicine, which didn't sit well with me. Slapping my arm, the old lady mumbled under her breath, "Why don't village people trust us?"

Rolling my eyes, I looked away. "Maybe because you lie about your practices," I whispered.

Stopping her hand midway to my arm, she frowned. "What was that?"

Smiling, I shook my head. "Nothing."

Shaking her head, she pressed the cloth hard on my scraped skin, causing me to hiss in pain.

Once all my cuts were cleaned, I was finally able to leave. Since training was over and the rest of the Riders were out on patrol, I had nothing to do. I debated about going to practice once more, but as I moved my arm, the pain had me thinking twice. Instead, I decided to take a tour around the castle. I had only been here for four days, and still no one had shown me round. The only areas I knew were my chambers and the direction to the training fields.

Walking down the spiral staircase from the healer's room, I took notice of all the markings on the wall. They were the same markings the lady had on her forehead. "She must really want to keep something out," I whispered.

More like someone, a sudden voice said.

Looking around, as if someone was going to pop out of nowhere, I was met with silence. There was no one around me. Looking back where I had come, again I was met with silence. "Hello?"

Moving my gaze back to the landing platform of the stairs, I hoped to see someone there, but it was empty. Moving towards one of the windows along the wall, I frowned. "Who is this? Why are you in my head?"

So many questions, and none that can be answered.

Frowning, I shook my head. "Tell me who this is."

I am the High Priest. Have you forgotten my voice already, Rider Abagail?

Eyes wide, I thought back to the first day in the castle. I had been bathing when the same voice entered my mind. As

I gazed at one of the symbols near my head, I frowned. "Tell me who the healer is trying to keep out."

Look outside and your answers will greet you.

Turning to gaze outside the window, I spotted someone walking towards the thick forest. Squinting to get a better look, a gasp left my lips when the person turned around. "Princess Anna?" I whispered. "But why is she…?"

Follow her. Quickly!

Rushing down the stairs, I gripped the rail, swinging myself around the corner and to the door. Seeing me rushing towards the door, one of the soldiers opened it for me with a small, confused nod. Not wasting any time, I rushed towards the tree-line.

Stealth will keep you safe. Safe is your way home to your bed.

Following her words, I crept through the thick forest. The sun had already started to set, casting the trees in a dark hue of orange and red. I had never been in the forest at this time before, and it made my heart sink as I thought about how my father must have felt.

Gritting my teeth, I pushed those thoughts out of my mind. I needed to find Anna. It was getting dark and who knew if rogues were out here. She could have been in danger. Or worse, she could be walking into a trap. As I walked deeper, the sound of voices off to the left caught my attention. It sounded like Anna, but the other person I couldn't pinpoint.

Creeping behind a fallen tree trunk, I peered over the edge. Squinting, I could make out Anna standing with a dark hooded figure. His voice was deep and rough, but it seemed so familiar. It was like I had heard his voice before, but didn't know where. Moving along the tree to get closer, I listened.

"Well? Did you do as I asked?"

"It wasn't easy to break through her hold with the dragon, but I was able to bring them down from the sky," Anna said.

Taking a step closer, the man's voice deepened. "I gave you orders to kill her."

Stepping back with hands raised, Anna shook her head. "I swear I tried, but I couldn't break through…" He cut her off with a slap on the cheek, and Anna whimpered as she gently placed her hand on the mark.

"Please, I'll try harder. I promise."

Gripping her chin in his hand, the man took a step closer. "I'll give you one more chance. Don't take this lightly, Anna, or your requests, along with yourself, will vanish."

Frowning, I moved forward, but the sound of a twig snapping under my foot had me freezing.

Abagail? Aurora whimpered.

She could feel the fear that was now creeping through my veins.

Holding out his hand, the hooded man started chanting in a language I hadn't heard before. As he closed his hand, a gust of wind knocked me hard onto the ground. At the impact with the uneven forest floor, I felt the air leave my lungs. My side burned, as the feeling of warm liquid rushed down my arm.

Sitting up, I struggled to draw in a breath. Groaning, I gripped my side. "Aurora," I spat out. Hissing, I staggered to my feet. As I gazed at the spot where Anna and the man had been just seconds ago, I was speechless. "What?" I whispered. No one was there. It was as if I had imagined everything; but the pain in my side was a reminder that it was real.

The sound of a roar off in the distance had my racing heart slowing. "Aurora?"

I'm not far away.

Walking further in the direction Anna had been, I gazed at the ground. There was no trace of anyone even being here. The ground held no footprints, with the leaves resting untouched on their spots – but something caught my eye. A black object had been abandoned on the ground. Carefully bending down, I picked it up.

"A book?" Turning over the book, I expected to see a title, but the cover was bare. Opening the book, I looked at its contents. It was in a language I had never seen before. It wasn't something I had been shown by my mother, or something we had spoken about back at the village. There were a bunch of symbols with written descriptions, and the longer I looked at it the more I noticed how some of the symbols resembled the markings on the healer's forehead.

Landing with a loud thud behind me, Aurora puffed out through her nose. *What happened?*

Shaking my head, I continued to gaze at the book. "I don't know." Staggering to my feet, I turned around, with the book raised in my hand. Flickering her gaze to the book, Aurora's body language changed. Hunching down in a threatening manner, she let out a deep growl.

Where did you find this?

"Anna. She was talking to a hooded man and…"

Lowering her body to the ground, she growled once more as she looked around us. *That wasn't just any hooded man... nor is that just any book, Abagail.*

Frowning, I lowered the book to my side. "What is this, Aurora?"

That is the book of dark spells. Used by King Toban himself.

"I need to give this to the king." Walking back towards the castle, I wasn't sure how I'd be able to tell him.

What are you doing?

Turning round, I frowned at Aurora. "He needs to know his daughter is conversing with the Dark King."

Landing in front of me, Aurora spread out her wings in some way to stop me. *We don't know anything for certain.*

Holding the book tighter in my hand, I raised it. "Did you not just say this book is used by the Dark King?"

Frowning, Aurora lowered her wings. *Yes, I did. But if you accuse the princess of such crimes, you will be sent to the dungeons. Who do you think they will believe first?*

Groaning, I looked down at the black-covered book. It was old, with the once-white pages stained an odd brown colour. Aurora was right. If I rushed in to see the king, they would think I was trying to harm the princess. After all, I was just a mere girl who found luck. They would never believe me.

Gritting my teeth, I shook my head. "Then what do you suppose I do with the book?"

Moving to my side, Aurora gently rubbed her head against my own. *You wait. But for now, we rest.*

Shaking my head, I looked at the castle doors. "I can't just let this go, Aurora!"

And we won't. We must keep an eye on the princess. If she is using dark magic, then she could be the one who made my vision go black.

Fifteen

I was awake before the sun the very next day. I hadn't been able to sleep after what happened in the woods. I kept playing over the events that had occurred. The words the Dark King chanted stuck in my brain, my mouth whispering its words as I drifted to sleep.

When I woke, I found myself continuing that chant. I couldn't get it out of my head. No matter what I did, I kept whispering the words over and over. Taking a deep breath, I lifted my bow, aiming it at the target off in the distance. The sun was starting to make itself known, turning the trees a light shade of orange.

Gritting my teeth, I found myself chanting the words again. "*Thúl n- nin polod.*" Releasing my finger, I watched the arrow sail through the air with a loud whistle. Hitting the target at full force, it exploded. Gasping, I lowered my bow. "What?" I hissed.

Dropping the bow, I ran towards the target. It was destroyed. Its painted face laid in pieces on the grass, wood splinters sticking out of the ground. A loud thud behind me caused me to jump.

Standing behind me, Aurora frowned at the target. *What did you chant, Abagail?*

Swallowing the growing lump in my throat, I bit my bottom lip. "I don't know," I whispered. Turning back round, I looked for the arrow. Sticking out of the ground, it seemed to be in perfect condition.

Shaking my head, I bent down to grab the arrow, but paused. "I just said what that man chanted."

Aurora growled. *You used dark magic.*

"Well, I didn't think this would happen," I said. Gesturing to the target, I stood up. "How was I meant to know this was going to happen?"

Shaking her giant head, she moved closer. *When you used that magic, I felt nothing but evil flow through my veins.* Laying on her stomach, she gently nudged my mark with her nose. *Everything you do, Abagail, flows through me. I hear your thoughts, feel your pain. When you use magic, I feel that too.*

"So you knew what I chanted?"

Nodding her head, she closed her eyes.

You used evil.

Galad will peni- cin lain.

"Did you hear that?" I asked.

Shaking her head, Aurora frowned. *Hear what?*

Moving closer to her, I lowered my voice. "Since I came here, I've heard another voice," I said. "When I left the healer's chambers, I was told to look out the window." Moving my hands to the forest, I moved closer to Aurora. "That's how I knew Anna was in there."

Turning her head slightly, Aurora went silent. Growling, she lowered her head towards the ground.

Someone is coming.

Looking behind her giant body, I spotted Matthew walking towards us. His hands were behind his back, his long hair down, casting a dark shadow over his face. I noticed he was dressed in his Rider clothes. Dark red with white trim. On his shoulders was scaled armour.

Looking at Aurora, he nodded, before looking back at me. "There is a meeting in the grand hall. You are required to change before it starts."

Frowning, I tilted my head. "Change into what?"

Smirking, he nodded at what I was wearing. It was nothing special, just brown leathers trousers and a crisp, white, long-sleeve shirt.

"You can't wear common clothes to a meeting with the king. Your armour has been sent to your chamber." With that said, he turned and walked away.

Aurora growled as she watched him walk towards the castle doors. *I don't trust him.*

"Why is that?" I questioned. Turning to face her, I watched her gaze follow Matthew.

I just feel something is off with him. Be careful.

Nodding, I patted her side, before following Matthew into the castle.

Arriving at my chamber, I was shocked to see my armour. I had thought it would look like the suits worn by the other Riders, but what was laid out on my bed was nothing close to that. It was a light blue dress, fully open at the legs. Accompanying the dress were tight dark blue leather trousers. Around the waist was a scaled armoured piece that resembled Aurora's scales. As I gripped the fabric in my hands, I noticed that there were no sleeves or shoulder straps.

"You need to show your mark."

Gasping at the sudden voice, I spun around. Leaning against the frame of my door was William. He was once again dressed in his white suit, gold trim decorating the edges. Around the cuffs was scaled armour. Smiling, I focused on my Rider armour. "I thought I would be dressed like all of you."

"No." Walking into my chambers, he looked around. As I gazed at the fabric, I heard his intake of air. "The meeting will start shortly." With that, he left. I couldn't help but get the feeling he wanted to say something else. Shaking the thoughts from my mind, I focused on dressing for the meeting.

Rushing down the hall to the great room, I started to panic. I had gotten lost. Actually, *lost* was an understatement. I had ended up on the other side of the castle. If it had not been for one of the lady's maids, I would never have known where to go.

Skidding to a stop in front of the grand door, I took a deep breath. I nodded at the guards, and they opened the doors. Chatter instantly filled my ears. I was late. Flinching slightly as the talking stopped, I lifted my gaze to see all eyes on me. All nine Riders were gazing at me. The king looked at me with no emotion. He looked stressed, and as my gaze moved to William, I noticed his smirk. He was enjoying this.

Gritting my teeth, I plastered a smile on my face. Walking to the edge of the round table, I bowed. "I'm sorry, Your Highness. I had gotten lost in your home."

Smiling warmly up at me, he bowed his head slightly. "That is fine, Rider. Take your seat."

Still hunched over, I lifted my head. The king's hand was raised, palm facing me. Standing straight, I walked to my chair beside Talios. Clearing his throat, the king stood. Walking towards the giant map situated in the middle of the table, he pushed a small icon towards one of the little villages.

"Noblemen Country was attacked last night," he hissed.

"Were there any casualties?" Talios rumbled.

Shaking his head, King Albert sighed in relief. "Thankfully, their town soldiers were able to fight off the rogues."

At the mention of rogues, I felt my skin crawl as a chill ran down my back. My hand ached where the blade had connected with my skin, the tissue still trying to heal itself.

"I want to send a few Riders there as a reassurance. Let them know we will stop at nothing to keep them safe." Walking back to his throne, King Albert sank down into the plush red fabric. "Four Riders will be scouting a nearby forest. Word has gone out that there is a camp near the town."

"Who shall be leaving?" asked William.

Smiling, King Albert looked around the table, his eyes gazing at the Riders before him. "I will be sending the best Riders to scout the forest." Linking his hands together, he smiled. "Rider Talios, Rider Reeve and Rider Vicar, you will be scouting the forest." Turning to William, he grasped his son on the shoulder. "I want you to take Rider Markus, Rider Matthew, and our newest Rider to the village."

"What?" Talios yelled. "You want to send someone who can't protect the people, let alone themselves, to a village that was attacked by rogues no longer than a day ago?"

Raising his hands to silence the chatter, William stood, staring down the men at the table. "Rider Abagail has shown herself more than once in front of me. Did she not become the first person to end the fighting at her ceremony?" Glancing at Talios, his gaze hardened. "If I recall, Talios, you did not defeat the Riders."

Frowning, Talios slammed his fist onto the table. "That is beyond the point. You can't have a girl."

"Who is a Rider just like you," said King Albert. Getting to his feet, he frowned. "I do not care that she has only just become a Rider. She proved to me her skills." Turning to me, he smiled. "You will be going to the village to greet the people, and reassure them you are there to help."

Smiling at him, I bowed. "Thank you, Your Highness. I will not let you down."

Sixteen

Once we arrived at Noblemen Country, I was shocked and repulsed by the sight before me. I knew this area wasn't the nicest of places to visit, but I hadn't imagined it would look like this.

Fog covered most of the village; its only source of light was from the many lanterns hung on buildings. The gravel roads were littered with rotting food, with some children scavenging through wooden crates. Their clothes were old and dirty, some children not even wearing shoes.

Closing my eyes, I took a deep breath. I had to remind myself why I was here. I couldn't be thinking about their living situation or their struggle for food. I was here to do a job.

Walking beside me, his hand gripping his sword, William lowered his voice. "I want you to take this." Holding out his hand, I noticed he was holding my bow. Gazing up at him in shock, I saw him smiling down at me. "Your mother left if after your ceremony."

Smiling, I grabbed my father's bow. "Thank you," I whispered. Now I felt complete. Without my father's bow, I felt like something was missing.

Patting my shoulder, he smiled, before walking ahead of me. "Keep an eye out. This place is full of thieves."

Placing my arm through the gap of the bow, I slung it over my shoulder. Tying the quiver to my hip, I nodded. William was right. The people of this town came from well-known villages, but left once they committed a horrible crime.

Taking a deep breath, I steadied my nerves. "Tell Aurora to scout from the skies," William ordered.

Nodding, I turned to my dragon. "Please let me know if you see something."

Bowing her head, she turned to leave. *Just be careful, Abagail.*

"I will," I whispered.

Walking through the town, I couldn't help but feel like I was being watched. In my Rider uniform, I stood out from the people here, with some even stopping their actions to gossip. Clenching my fists, I continued down the path.

Nothing seemed to be out of place. There was a small market with some ladies selling fruit that looked to be rotting. Playing around the carts were small children; their clothes were worn and tattered. As I watched the boys play, I felt a heated gaze to my left.

Turning towards the direction I felt the stare, I noticed Matthew looking at me. His eyebrows were furrowed, a far-off look on his face, but that wasn't what caught my eye. On his left cheek was a deep cut.

"Aurora, did Rider Matthew have a cut when we landed?" I whispered.

No, he was unscathed.

Something wasn't right with him. Frowning, I watched as he moved between two huts. Taking after him, I gripped my bow tighter. I had a bad feeling he was up to no good. As I rounded a small hut, he was nowhere to be seen. "Dammit!" I hissed. The sound of a rock moving made me freeze. Snapping my head in that direction, I felt my body go taut. The air was knocked out of my chest, and tears instantly pooled in my eyes.

"Papa?" I whispered.

As I turned around, the man quickly ran down the path. Gripping my bow, I ran after him. Dodging the townspeople, I gritted my teeth as I tried to push my legs to move faster. "Papa!" I yelled, tears streaming down my face. "Stop there now!"

He halted in his tracks, and I grabbed my bow, aligning an arrow with the string. Pulling it back, I aimed at the man. "Turn around," I whispered. He shook his head at my request, only adding to my anger. "Turn around!" Breathing heavily, I waited for the man to turn.

Placing his hands in the air, I watched his head shake. "Turn around now!" I screamed. A few of the townspeople stopped to watch the scene, but I paid no attention to them. My main focus was on the man who looked like my father. There was no way he could be real – he died. I know he did.

"Abagail!" Markus shouted to my left. Running towards me, Markus gripped my wrist that held the string back. "Abagail, lower your weapon." Shaking my head, I blinked away the tears.

"Turn around," I whispered, defeated.

Lowering his hands, the man in front of me slowly turned around. Gasping in shock, I felt my tears fall.

Lowering my weapon, I gazed at my father. Shaking my head, I took a deep breath. "You died."

Shaking his head, he went to move forward, but stopped when I held out my hand. This couldn't be real. The man in front of me looked so much like my father. His hair was short, with dirt covering his stubbly cheeks. Shaking my head, I stepped back. "N-no. You died!" I screamed.

Gently gripping my arm, Markus pulled me towards him. "Abagail. Let him explain."

Frowning at Markus, suddenly everything made sense. "You knew?"

Lowering his head, he nodded. "I found him here on my first patrol."

"Abagail, darling, let me explain," Father whispered. Moving towards me, I watched as a tear fell down his cheek.

"No!" I screamed. "You left us!"

Running towards me with a frown, he gripped my arm with a shake of his head. "I never wanted to, I swear."

Pulling my arm away from his grip, I glared up at him. "Mother and I mourned for you." Gritting my teeth, I threw my bow on the ground. "I mourned for you!" Untying the arrows from my waist, I threw the quiver at his feet. "I mourned for a father that wasn't really dead."

"I did it for you!" Gripping my arms, he squeezed them gently. "I did it to protect you from him."

Shaking my head, I stepped back, the feeling of my father's touch still lingering on my skin. I had dreamed of being held by him again, and now it repulsed me. Blinking away the blur in my vision, I frowned. "You're a coward."

"Abagail, let him explain," Markus whispered.

"No!" Pushing Markus away from me, I watched as he flew backwards into a cart full of apples. Grunting at the impact, Markus looked up at me. "I'm sorry," I mumbled, blinking the tears away. I couldn't be here. Turning round, I ran back to the clearing we had landed in, leaving the shouts of my father behind me.

"Aurora!" The sound of her scream filled my ears. Flying over my head, she landed only a few feet away from me. "Take me home." Climbing on her back, I gripped at the saddle. "Take me away from here."

Of course.

"Abagail, stop!" Markus and William were running towards me, their hands on their weapons. Shaking my head, I kicked my heels into Aurora's side. With a growl, she shot up into the sky, leaving them behind.

Sitting on the cliff back at Knights Edge, I watched as the sun descended over the land. The castle view was off in the distance, but this time no dragons were flying around. The air was still. There was no breeze, no sounds of birds chirping, nothing. Something didn't feel right.

Leaning against Aurora, I gazed at my surroundings. I felt that something bad was coming for us soon. We needed to be prepared.

Looking at her, I watched her eyes twitch. She was scanning the area. Moving closer to her body, I closed my eyes. I felt exhausted from the day's events. Finding my father still alive left me feeling empty all over again. I had left the bow and arrows behind, leaving me without a weapon.

Sleep, Rider, as the evil will come for us soon.

Seventeen

"You disobeyed orders!"

The king's voice boomed through the throne room. A few of the High Priest's followers frowned down at me. I was currently kneeling down in front of King Albert in his throne room. When I had landed on the castle grounds, knights had arrested me, before bringing me to him.

Word of my leave from the mission had spread through the castle like wild fire. A few of the lady's maids had frowned at me as I was dragged through the halls. When I arrived at the throne room, William and Anna were standing beside their father. The look on William's face had my heart dropping. He looked disappointed in me, whereas Anna had a smirk. Gritting my teeth as pain shot up through my knees, I tried to think of something else.

"Do you not feel remorse?" asked the king.

"Father." Rising to his feet, William frowned. "She just found her father, who she thought to be dead."

"I do not care for such things! She is a Rider before anything else." Moving down the steps towards me, King Albert stopped only inches from my face. "You shall be punished for your actions."

Snapping my head up to him, I could see he was struggling. His face was twisted with different emotions. He had to make an example out of me in front of everyone, and I could understand that. After all, I did run away from a task given to me. Lifting his head high, his voice boomed throughout the hall. "You are banned from flying till I say otherwise."

William stood from his seat. "But, Your High…"

"You will not be going on any more patrols either."

Taking a sharp breath, I nodded. "As you wish," I whispered.

Walking back to his throne, King Albert sat down with a sigh. "This is for your own good, Abagail." He sighed again. Lowering my gaze, I nodded. "Take her back to her room, William."

"Yes, Father." Gripping my arm, William hauled me to my feet.

Stumbling as he dragged me out of the room, I tried to fight back the tears. It had only been a week since I had arrived, and already I had been punished for my actions. I could hear Aurora's whine in the back of my head, and I felt guilty. Not only was I being punished, but so was she. Not being able to fly would be torture for her.

Once we arrived at my room, I sat on my bed. William stood by the closed door, hands in his trousers pocket. He hadn't said a word since we left the throne room.

Gazing up at him, I tightened my fists by my sides, clenching the soft fabric between my fingers. "I'm sorry."

Sighing, he shook his head. "I would've done the same."

"You would?" I couldn't take him as someone who would disobey his father's orders. If he did, I'm sure he'd be exiled for treason.

Sitting down beside me with a sigh, he lowered his head. "What you did was stupid on your part. But I can understand why you did it." Turning to me, a sad smile graced his face. "It must've been hard for you. Seeing your father after all this time must've been traumatic."

Glancing at my hands, I tried to fight the tears that threatened to fall. All this time, I had mourned for my father, and yet he was still alive. Wrapping his arms around my shoulder, I felt his hand gently push my head to his shoulder.

"It's okay to cry, Abagail," he whispered. Gritting my teeth, I let the tears fall. The tears of betrayal and hate rolled down my cheeks. Tightening his hold around me, he muttered soothing words near my ear.

The next morning rain fell from the sky. It was almost like it knew how I was feeling. Laying in the warm water of my bath, I closed my eyes and connected myself with Aurora.

You seem better.

Sinking lower into the warm water, I whispered, "As well as I can be."

Are you going to tell your mother?

"I'd rather not hurt her any more than what she is right now." Opening my eyes, I gazed at the stone wall. "She mourned far worse than I did. I don't want to give her another reason to cry again."

Very well.

Closing my eyes once more, I disconnected myself from Aurora. The feeling of energy leaving my body left tingles in its wake. Rotating my neck, I sighed. The silence of the bathing room was odd. Usually, there were lady's maids rushing around, or the sound of the water falling from the rock walls… but there was nothing.

Gazing around the room, I listened. There were no sounds. All the other Riders had gone back to Noblemen Country at sunrise, due to rogue sightings a couple of miles out from the town. Because I was being punished for my actions, it also meant I wasn't allowed to know any details. William, though, had told me everything. He believed what I did wasn't punishable, and I should have been excused for my actions. Nonetheless, I was willing to follow the king's orders.

After dressing in my Rider uniform, I decided to go visit Aurora. I could feel her getting restless with not being allowed to fly, which only made me feel worse.

Heading down the spiral staircase, I turned down a hallway that led towards the field. Stepping out from a door on the left, Matthew pulled a hood over his head.

Shocked by his sudden appearance, I hid behind a wall. I had thought all Riders were at Noblemen Country. He shouldn't be here. "Aurora, is Matthew's dragon here?" I whispered. I waited for her reply.

No, his dragon is gone.

"What is he up to?" I whispered. Peeking out from the wall, I watched as he looked around the area, before walking out to the field. Frowning, I moved towards the door he had come from.

"Strange... This door is usually guarded." Pushing open the door, I peered in. Through the door was a small corridor that led to a spiral staircase. Following the staircase all the way up, it led to another door; but what caught my attention was all the markings.

"Aurora, are you seeing this?" I whispered. There was no reply. "The markings must be stopping me." Walking up to the door, I ran my finger over the marking on the door. It was in a spiral pattern that looked like my mark. Pushing open the door, I peered inside. In the middle of the dimly lit room was a book. Taking a deep breath, I gazed at the book. "Why is this book floating?"

Finally, you have come, echoed a voice.

"Who's there?" Clenching my fists, I waited for someone to step out from the shadows. "I'm warning you now... show yourself!"

Have you forgotten my voice already, Abagail?

Turning my head towards the floating book, I couldn't help but frown. "High Priest?"

I'm known as the Priestess of the Dragons... I am the original Priest.

Stepping closer, I gazed at the book. It was different to the one I had seen before. "But I thought what the Priest had in Knights Edge was the great book."

That is a decoy... I cannot leave the confinements of this room.

"Why can't you leave?" The pages of the book opened, causing it almost to glow as it stopped on an empty page.

If I am taken, so will the new Dragon Riders.

"Who would take you?"

Evil... evil was here trying to get in before.

"Matthew!" I hissed. "Why was he here?"

You must protect those you love, as evil will be here... Soon.

The sound of the dragons' roars echoed through the dark room. They were back, which meant William was, too. Rushing down the spiral staircase, I ran out of the room, making sure the door was closed behind me.

Running out to the open field, I saw that William was laughing with a few of the Riders, including Markus. Grabbing William's arm, I pulled him away from the group.

"What's wrong?" Gazing down at me, William frowned. "I thought you were staying in your room?"

"I need your help," I said.

Nodding, William gazed at the group off to the side. "What's wrong?"

"I know about the great book."

Frowning, he shook his head. "Everyone knows about the great book, Abagail. Where are you...?"

"Not the fake one the Priestess' followers carry... I know, William."

Instantly, his face paled. Looking around, he gripped my arm. "How did you find it?"

"Matthew came out through the door."

"That door is meant to be locked and guarded," he hissed.

"Well, it wasn't... I watched him walk from that room."

"And you thought you'd go in."

"Wouldn't you? It's not the first time I've had a strange feeling about him. Back at Noblemen Country, I watched him walk out of a hut with carvings on the door."

"Carvings?"

Licking my lips, I sighed. "Something isn't right with him."

Clenching his jaw, William watched as the Riders walked back into the castle. "He wasn't on patrol either."

"And yet his dragon wasn't here," I said. "Let's go talk somewhere else, okay?"

He nodded, and I led him to my chambers. Closing the door behind us, I turned to see William gazing at something on my bed. Picking it up, he turned to me with a frown.

"Why is there a dark spells book on your bed?"

Eighteen

"Let me explain!" As I went to reach for the book, he moved away. As he shook the book in his hands, with gritted teeth I watched his eyes change colour. "William, stop." Gently grasping the tops of his arms, I gave them a gentle squeeze.

Closing his eyes, his jaw flexed. "Tell me how it got here."

Sighing, I moved away. Sitting on the bed, I gazed down at my hands. "I found it in the woods after following someone."

"Who?"

Taking a deep breath, I prepared myself. Telling William about his sister wasn't a good idea, but if I didn't, he would hate me. Since being here, he was the only person on my side. Not even Markus had stood up for me. Hell, he knew about my father being alive and didn't tell me.

"Anna... I followed Anna into the woods."

Throwing the book on the ground, William stalked closer to me. "And she had this on her?"

"No, I didn't see her with this, but..."

"So you're blaming my sister without proof?"

Shaking my head, I rose from the bed. "She was talking to a man in a cape. His hood was covering his face, so I couldn't see him, but I think it was Matthew."

Clenching his fists, he turned and punched the wall. Gasping in shock, I stepped back, until I noticed the blood on his hands. Stepping towards him, I gently grasped his wrist. "You're hurt."

"Why didn't you tell me this before, Abagail?" he whispered.

Lowering my head, I gazed at his wound. "I didn't think anyone would believe me... besides, as it is I've already become the worst Dragon Rider in history."

Turning to me, William gently grasped my chin. Lifting my head so I could meet his gaze, he frowned. "My sister isn't a good person, Abagail, but she wouldn't do this... I know she wouldn't."

"What can I do for you to believe me?"

"She isn't a bad person, Abagail... I know she isn't."

Pulling my chin from his grip, I stepped away. I knew he wouldn't believe me; it was his sister, after all. But Matthew, I knew, was up to no good. "Then it must be Matthew."

Opening his mouth to speak, he stopped when the sound of running feet echoed through the hall. Bursting open the door, guards ran into my room. Grasping my arms, they pulled me away from William. "What is going on!" shouted William.

"She is to be taken to the dungeons." As we turned towards the voice, King Albert and Anna walked in, a priest not too far behind.

"What is the meaning of this, Father?"

Holding out his hand to one of the guards, the King grabbed the black book in his hand. "She has been using dark magic like the townspeople thought."

"I told you I found the book on her bed." Anna sneered.

"What?" Trying to shake the grip on my arms, I tried to move towards her. She was setting me up. "You lie!" Gritting my teeth, I used all the energy I could to break the hold. "You are setting me up!"

"Riders!"

Rushing into the room, Markus and Talios took me from the guards.

"And here I thought you were good," whispered Talios.

Tears filled my eyes as I continued to glare at Anna. "Why are you doing this? I'm not the one you should be taking. Anna was the one talking to a hooded man in the forest!"

"She lies, Father; don't believe her."

Nodding, King Albert looked at Markus and Talios. "Take her to a cell."

"What?" This couldn't be happening. Gritting my teeth, I tapped into Aurora's strength.

"Healer!" shouted the king.

Rushing to his father's side, William pleaded, "Father, don't do this."

"She will be our downfall if we don't stop her now." The king nodded at the old lady who had walked into the room, and she moved behind me. The feeling of pressure on the back of my neck was the last thing I felt, before everything went black.

The sound of dripping water stirred me from my sleep. Pain in my neck had me wincing, as I tried to move from my spot. Taking a deep breath, I winced at the foul smell. Opening my eyes, I looked around.

"You have to be kidding," I whispered. Rolling over to my side, I tried to sit up. Around me were dark-coloured walls: mould seemed to be growing on them from the water that dripped from above.

Leaning against the wall, I winced as the mould wet my back. Hissing at the cold touch, I gritted my teeth. Closing my eyes, I tapped into Aurora.

You are finally awake.

"What's happening?" I whispered.

They believe you are working against the king.

"That's not true." Gritting my teeth, I tried to stand. My whole body felt stiff. Nothing felt right. Whatever that healer did to me, my body wasn't agreeing with it.

Walking to the iron bars, I gripped them tight. Nobody was around here. I thought, at the very least, maybe a few soldiers would be standing guard, but there was no one.

"Hello!" I tried to get someone's attention. This wasn't right. Anna was manipulating them. She was the one who was working with Toban, not me. "Let me out of here!"

It was no use; no one was coming down here. Sighing, I walked back to the corner. Sitting down, I tried to stop my body from shaking.

Right now, I wished I was back in the fields with my mother. I wanted to go back to hunting. I wanted to have Alex laugh at me for trying to act like the male of the town. I wanted to go back to the old me who dreamed of meeting Markus again.

Closing my eyes to stop the tears from falling, I clenched my hands into tight fists. "It wasn't me."

Nineteen

Walking down the spiral staircase, I pushed open the door that led to the great book. Floating in the middle of the room, the book glowed a bright white as a soft hum came from it. Walking closer to the book, I ran my hands over the cover. The roughness of the gold leather scraped against my skin. Grabbing the book in my hands, I pulled it towards me. The glow died down as I placed the book on the floor.

Gripping the sword at my side, I whispered, *"Gurth na i aran plural erain or erein."* Lifting my sword, I brought it down onto the middle of the book…

Sitting up on the concrete floor, I gasped for air as pain hit me in the chest. I found it hard to breathe as I gripped my shirt. Groaning, I crawled towards the bars. Sitting off to the side was a guard. His feet were planted atop a small wooden table, his head lolled back. Gripping onto the bars of the cell tighter, I gritted my teeth.

"Help," I whispered. "Please." After waiting a few minutes, I shook my head. "Guard!" I yelled. Snapping his head in my direction, he saw me collapse onto my back. "Help!"

Rushing to my side, the guard yelled for help. As my cell door opened, I heard a few more footsteps, followed by my name being called. Opening my eyes, I gazed up into William's concerned face. "What's happening?" Turning to the guard, he frowned. "What did you do?"

"I didn't do anything. I was just sitting there when she called for help."

Clutching my chest, I let out a scream as the pain became too much to hold back. Gripping my hand, William leaned over me. "What's wrong?"

"The book," I whispered. "The Great Book."

I watched his face staring at me, then pinch before realisation hit him. Turning to one of the guards, he barked out orders. "Head to the Great Book now, and take your men!"

Jumping to his feet, the soldier rushed towards the stairs that led to the main floor of the castle. Pulling me towards his body, William held me near his chest. "How?" he whispered loud enough for me to hear.

"Dream," I gritted out.

Tightening his grip on me, he looked around.

"We need to move her," said one of the soldiers.

"Get the healer."

"No! Go to the book now!" I said through gritted teeth. Turning to one of the men, he nodded.

Getting to his feet, the soldier dashed out of the room and up the stairs. Moving his focus back to me, William bent down. Picking me up, he walked towards the stairs. "Run to the healer and let her know that we are coming."

"Yes, my prince."

I watched as the soldier ran ahead of us and disappeared out of sight. Gasping at the pain in my chest, I gripped onto William's shirt. The soft fabric was smooth against my skin. Once we reached the healer's room, I was placed on the bed. Walking to my side, the elderly lady placed her hand on my forehead. A gasp ripped out of her lips as her head shot backwards.

"The sight," she whispered. Looking down at me, she frowned. "The book." Turning to William, her eyes widened. "Send someone to the Great Book now!"

"I've already sent one of my men there."

Shaking her head, she rushed around the room. "The book isn't safe; you must protect it."

Moving to my side, William frowned. "What do you mean?"

"The book is tied to this girl!" she yelled. Shaking her head with a frown, she grabbed a bottle off the shelf. It was blue in colour and as she pulled the lid off, a foul smell came from the liquid inside. It smelt like a combination of death and swamp water.

Dipping her finger into the liquid, she moved towards me. Brushing my hair off my face, she began to draw a symbol on my forehead.

"What are you doing?" asked William.

"I'm trying to protect the Rider," she mumbled. Once she was done, she pulled back. "This will help with the pain."

Taking a deep breath, I felt the pain in my chest disappear. "What was that?"

"It's a blocking symbol. It's to block your ties with the Great Book." After placing the bottle back on the shelf by her window, I watched as she started pacing back and forth. "This doesn't make sense," she whispered.

I agreed with her. None of this made sense. Since I met Aurora, I've had nothing but weird stuff happen to me. Sighing, I closed my eyes. I tried to channel Aurora, but when nothing happened, I frowned.

"Why can't I sense Aurora?"

"The symbol will block your connection with her. You are all tied together to that book, and I'm unsure as to why." Walking to a bookshelf at the far end of the room, she ran her fingers across the books. When she found the one, the healer pulled it out. I watched her open it to a certain page and her eyes scanned the contents.

"It's really rare for something like this to happen."

The sound of footsteps rushing towards us caught my attention. Stopping at the door, one of the soldiers gasped for air.

"The book is gone!" he huffed.

Gritting his teeth, William gripped the handle of his sword. "What's gone?"

"The book and the princess are gone."

When I walked into the meeting room, all the Riders were seated around the large oak table. At the head of the table was King Albert. His head was resting against his hands, his shoulders hunched forward. As I made my way to my seat next to Rider Talios, I noticed Matthew's tense figure.

He sat stock still on his chair. His eyes roamed around the room as if a rogue was about to jump out. Sitting down in front of him, I kept my gaze on his body.

"She's gone," whispered the king.

Tilting his head, Markus frowned. "Who's gone?"

"Princess Anna."

Gritting his teeth, Markus slapped his hands onto the table. "Then what are we doing here?" Rising to his feet, he went to move, but was stopped by William. "You aren't the only one who wants her back; but we can't go rushing into the Dark Kingdom."

"She could be getting hurt!" Markus screamed.

"Enough!" yelled King Albert. "She isn't the only one who is missing." Looking around the room, he sighed. "The Great Book is missing as well."

"How is that possible? That place is always guarded."

"We don't know. Rider Abagail informed us of something being wrong."

Turning to me, a few of the Riders frowned.

"She could be a spy for King Toban!" one Rider yelled.

"Agreed! How else would she know?"

"For she has the sight." Everyone turned towards the sound of the voice, as the elderly healer slowly walked towards the end of the table. "She came to me in pain. When I used my healing, I, too, could see what she saw."

Frowning, Talios turned to me. "How can we trust you? Every time something happens, you are involved."

Frowning, I stood. Gazing at the Riders around the table, I couldn't help but notice they all seemed to agree with Talios. Licking my lips, I nodded.

"I'll agree that I haven't been the best of Riders, but what do you expect? I was pushed into this life, not really knowing what I was getting myself into. After all, I'm the first female Rider in history, so I'm sorry if I haven't been acting like the rest of you."

Looking at Matthew, I frowned. He wasn't meeting my gaze. Instead, he chose to look down at the table. "If there is one thing I'm certain of… I would never put my kingdom or loved ones in harm's way." Tensing at my words, Matthew gazed up at me with a frown.

"I trust Abagail," William said simply. Moving towards his father, he looked over the men. "We must work together to find the Great Book and Anna."

Patting William on the back, King Albert stood. "I believe rogues may have her. Matthew has been speaking to one of our generals not too far from here."

"Where are the rogues?" asked Talios.

Moving to the map in the centre of the table, King Albert touched a clearing just off from the Dark Mountains. "General Mains has informed us of a rogues' camp deep in the mountains. The amount of rogues is unknown, but I believe that's where they've taken Anna."

"Then what are we still doing here?" Gripping the edge of the table, Markus breathed heavily through his nose.

"I want you all to get your things. We leave once everyone has gathered."

Rushing to their feet, the Riders moved out of the room. Moving to my side, the king gave me a small smile. "You are now free to ride."

Bowing to him, I smiled. "Let's find Princess Anna."

Patting my shoulder, the king nodded. "Go change and be ready – for we fly soon."

Rushing back to my room, I tried once again to contact Aurora. "Aurora?"

Finally, I can speak to you.

"I'm sorry." Looking around the hallway, I could see all the Riders rushing down towards the main floor. Walking into my room, I didn't care about closing the door as I changed into my uniform. "Did you hear about the Princess and the Great Book?"

Yes. You must be careful. I feel something bad is coming.

Twenty

As I made my way across the lush green field, I couldn't help but notice how stiff the air felt. No one was smiling, and as the lady's maids walked towards the safety of the castle, they didn't smile or laugh. I wasn't used to their silent nature. They would often laugh amongst one another, but now they walked with their heads down, with guards following their every move.

Gritting my teeth, I wiped my hands down the armour of my corset. Strapped around my waist was a quiver full of arrows, and my new bow made from dragon scales rested over my shoulder. It was heavier than my old bow, and just the thought of it brought back bad memories. Shaking my head, I rid my mind of those thoughts. I had to focus on the task at hand. The princess had been taken to god knows where, and the Great Book was missing. All I knew was someone with a sword had pierced the book, which in turn affected me. I had so many questions left unanswered, but as I rounded the corner of a brick building Aurora came into view.

She stood on all fours, legs spread wide in a show of dominance. A few of the other Riders watched as she shook her large body, the chain around her neck chiming as she did so. The chain was there to protect her from an attack. Considering we still had no idea of what we were facing, or if there were other Riders, I knew I'd have to do whatever it took to protect her.

You should be protecting yourself before me, Aurora whispered.

Looking up as her shadow fell over me, I noticed her face was coated in armour as well. Gold-plated armour made her bright blue eyes stand out. Smiling at her, I felt pride for the dragon. She was everything I had ever dreamt about, and knowing she was mine eased my thoughts.

"I will protect you first."

Then I shall do the same for you.

Lying down on the grass, Aurora lowered her wings to help me onto her back. It would only be the third time flying with Aurora, and this time it wasn't just for training. Walking to the white saddle on her back, I placed my foot through the strap.

The feeling of hands on my waist pushed me higher up the saddle so I could swing my legs over. Once seated, I turned to see who the hands belonged to. Smiling up at me was William. Although his smile didn't reach his eyes, he still offered me one to ease my mind.

Tightening the strap around Aurora's middle, he whispered, "Are you ready?"

Nodding my head, I offered him a smile. "We'll find her, William."

Stopping his actions, he looked up at me. Reaching down, I fixed the collar of his uniform, my hand gently brushing the skin on his neck. Smiling, he grabbed my hand in his, and I froze. I watched in pure shock as his lips gently touched the back of my hand. As he gazed back up at me, I saw his eyes twinkle with something new, something I hadn't seen in them before. It was almost like he was enjoying this.

"You just be careful." Releasing my hand, he took a step back. "Make sure you follow behind Talios and Markus. I'll see you at the camp."

Gripping the handle on the saddle, I nodded.

"Be safe." Bowing his head to me, he turned to Aurora. "Make sure you get her there safely."

Snorting, Aurora stood up to her full height. *You underestimate me.*

The sound of a few dragons' roars as they flew off had me gripping onto the saddle tighter.

"Let's ride!" shouted Talios. I watched as his green dragon shot up into the air, a scream released from its mouth.

"Follow, Abagail!" William shouted.

Nodding, I looked down at Aurora. "Let's go." Spreading her wings, I felt her body dip, before she shot up into the sky. The feeling of the wind stinging my skin had me biting down on my bottom lip. I still hadn't gotten used to the feeling, and as I closed my eyes to connect to Aurora, I slowly felt the pain disappear. Opening my eyes, I looked around the area. I couldn't see anything odd, but as we flew over a small village I hadn't known existed, I strained to look at the people who seemed to be running.

"What are they doing?" I whispered.

They are known as travellers. They don't stay in one place too long and come under no kingdom.

"So they don't care for the king?"

Looking away from the people, I couldn't help the frown that settled on my face. I couldn't imagine what life would be like constantly moving, having nowhere to really call home. All my life, I had called the village of Knights Edge my home, but now that I was at the castle it had become my new home.

As we came over a forest, I couldn't help but feel like something was watching us. Gazing down at the forest that passed underneath us, I could hear chanting.

Squinting my eyes, I willed my vision to change. The colours darkened and were replaced by heat. I could see animals grazing along the ground, but I could also see a group of people. As I passed over them, the chanting got louder. It was something I hadn't heard before.

The song of the Dark King, Aurora whispered.

Once we landed at the campsite, I took note of all the soldiers that were around. There had to be more than six hundred soldiers here, all wearing the royal army uniform of gold and white. Phoenix flags were hung around the camp, and off to the side were a group of soldiers practising combat skills. Situated in the middle of the camp was a giant firepit. Someone had stacked tree logs up, and I could only hope that when they lit it the rogues wouldn't see.

Jumping down from Aurora, I watched as William and his dragon landed a few feet away from me. Instantly, he was surrounded by soldiers and a man dressed in a general's uniform. I could only guess that this was General Mains. He was a young-looking man with orange hair. His face had a few freckles, and his eyebrows were furrowed as he spoke to William.

Making my way towards Markus, I noticed how tense he was. Even as he stood by his dragon, his whole body seemed to be stiff, as if he was expecting someone to jump out at him. Reaching his side, I placed my hand on his shoulder. Jumping back slightly by the contact, he spun around with a frown.

"Are you okay?" I asked.

He nodded, then cleared his throat. "I'm fine. I just want to find Anna already."

"We all do." Too bad I was lying. I didn't want her back. She was working for the Dark King, but even if I mentioned it to anyone, they wouldn't believe me, and I'd end up back in the cells.

Licking his bottom lip, his eyes darted around the field. "We just need to find her soon."

Moving away from him, I nodded. "We will."

Smiling down at me, he patted my shoulder, before moving towards William. "Come on, there is a meeting."

Following Markus towards a large tent, I noticed two guards standing either side of the tent, open hands placed on their swords. Frowning, I looked around. No one here seemed to be a threat, but then again, Matthew had appeared to be one from the moment I first met him. Ducking under the fabric, I headed towards an empty seat beside William.

We all sat around a circular table, a giant hand-drawn map situated in the middle. This one wasn't as detailed as the one back at the kingdom, but it was still very well drawn. All the cities and towns had been placed perfectly around the map, and a red dot had been placed off to the side.

Rising from his seat, William cleared his throat. Grabbing the red dot from the side, he placed it on the map. "Here is where a few patrols spotted the rogues," he said. "The amount of the force is unknown to us still, and the whereabouts of Princess Anna is still unknown, too."

"Do we know how far away the rogues are?" asked Rider Talios.

Taking a deep breath, William nodded. "We do." Moving the red dot into a thick forest about two days' walk away from here, he sighed. "We've had reports of sightings deep in the Dark Forest."

Leaning forward, I gazed at the marked spot. "How many?"

Looking up at William, I noticed a small smirk on his lips: it almost looked like his eyes were twinkling. Clearing his throat, he nodded towards the map. "We've had a report of at least a thousand rogues."

"We're outnumbered!" shouted Rider Leo.

Frowning, William gazed at the men in the room. "We may be outnumbered in men, but we have Riders. We can attack them from the sky and the ground."

Slamming his fist on the table, Talios stood to his full height. "There is still a low chance we will survive."

"Then we try our best," I said. Looking around the room, I noticed a few frowns on the men's faces. Gritting my teeth, I looked at the map. "If they are deep in the forest, why don't we cut them off?"

Scoffing, Talios shook his head. "You really think we would listen to you?"

"She is right," said Markus. Standing, he moved closer to the map. Using his finger, he drew a circle around the marker. "We can trap them with fire." Looking at the men, I noticed a few of them nodding. "The fire will trap them in, with nowhere to go."

Licking his lips, William sat down. "Then that's what we'll do. Talios, Markus and Leo will go first thing tomorrow morning and scout the area. Make sure you're at a height where they can't see you."

Nodding their heads, they bowed.

"Dismissed."

Twenty-One

"Abagail, wait!"

Turning round at the sudden shout, I spotted Markus running towards me. Gripping my arm, he pulled me between two tents, out of the view of the men around us. Leaning his head down, he touched his forehead with mine. I remember him doing this when we were little. The only times he'd do this was when he had done something bad and was about to ask for my forgiveness. Frowning, I placed a hand on his chest.

"What's wrong?" I whispered.

Shaking his head, he sighed. "I need you to go back to Knights Edge."

Shocked, I took a step back, my hand still resting on his chest. "What?"

He tried to take a step closer to me, but I frowned, and matched his step back.

"Please, I can't have you here if a war is going to break out."

"I'm a Rider, Markus; this is what I'm meant to do." I frowned up at him.

"But you're a *girl*."

Taken aback by his words, I removed the hand resting on his chest as if it had just caught fire. He had never brought that up before. He would always encourage me to do what I wanted, not have me running from a fight.

"Where is this coming from?" I asked with a frown. Opening his mouth to speak, he stopped, as voices neared us.

Standing at the edge of the tent was William, his lips parted slightly as he watched us with a frown. "Is something wrong here?" he asked.

Looking back at Markus' gaze on me, I shook my head. "No."

"Abagail." Reaching for my arm, I turned around and walked away. I didn't want to be there with him. His words had hurt me beyond what I thought they would. Was the reason they hurt because I still loved him? Shaking my head, I made my way to my marked tent. A few soldiers were guarding the entrance to the tent, swords held in their hands.

Walking towards them, I watched as they slightly raised their swords, before bowing their heads. They stepped out of the way and I was let into my tent. Inside was pretty empty. A stretcher bed was in the middle, a few change of clothes and my weapons. Sighing, I lay down on my bed, my mind going back to Markus.

I didn't understand why he was acting this way or what his motive was. The king needed all the soldiers here in order for the kingdom to be saved. If I were to run away from a problem again, I would be banished as a Rider and lose my mark. I didn't want to be known as that type of a person. Closing my eyes, I let my mind drift into nothingness.

***

Opening my eyes, I found myself in a dark room, the only source of light coming from a small window situated near the top of the roof. It was dark outside, causing the moon to shine an early blue glow into the room. Looking around, I noticed this room was covered in markings – ones not like anything I had seen before, but one marking on a door I especially noticed.

Frowning, I moved towards the door. Running my hand over the marking, a gasp escaped my lips as I fully focused on it.

"My mark," I whispered.

Spinning around, I headed to the middle of the room, where I saw a small book-stand. Sitting on the book-stand was the Great Book. The middle of the book had a hole, staining the pages in a dark blue colour. "The book's bleeding?"

I'm dying, my child.

Placing my hand flat over the book where the hole was, I felt a shock of electricity fly through my body..

Shooting up in bed, I looked around. Sitting on my bed with a frown was William. His hands were rested on my shoulders, brows furrowed together as he looked at my face.

"Are you okay?" he whispered.

Looking around the room, I nodded. "Yeah."

175

He took his hands away from my shoulder and I watched as the frown on his face deepened. "Was that another dream?"

Taking a deep breath, I nodded.

Biting my lip, I stared into his blue eyes. "It was the worst one yet," I whispered.

Taking another deep breath, I watched as he went to speak, but stopped when shouting outside caught us off-guard. Getting to his feet, he ran to the tent flap that led outside. Following after him, I pushed the flap back to see that it was now dark. The firepit was lit, and signs of a small feast could be seen around the fire, but now the camp was eerily quiet.

A few soldiers ran past me towards the woods, their weapons in hand. Following the men, I felt Aurora stirring. Something wasn't right. Walking around a tent, I noticed a large crowd had formed, and a few Riders sat on their dragons with frowns on their faces. Pushing my way through the crowd, I was shocked at who I saw was standing at the edge of the forest.

"Princess?" General Mains whispered in shock. Rushing towards her, he gripped the top of her arm.

Stepping towards William, I looked around at the men. I couldn't find Markus among the crowd. Surely, if Anna had suddenly appeared, he would want to be here, right? The thought of him being happy that his beloved Anna had returned caused bile to rise in my throat.

As I gazed at Anna, I couldn't help but get shivers. Something just didn't seem right with the way she was looking out at everyone. She almost seemed to have a smirk gracing her lips as the general ran towards her. She was enjoying the fuss over her.

As I watched Anna, something seemed to ring in my mind, as if someone or something was trying to reach me. "Aurora?" I whispered, as I gazed at the ground.

RUN! she shouted, before a loud roar filled the air.

Confused, I looked back at Anna, only to see a small smirk fall on her lips. Gripping William's arm, I slowly pulled him back towards me.

"Something isn't right," I whispered. I watched as his frown deepened. Sliding his arm through my grasp, he held onto my hand tightly. I watched as his eyes roamed the forest behind Anna. It was deadly silent; not a single noise was made.

Coming to a stop in front of Anna, General Mains gently grasped her arm. "Princess, are you all right?" he whispered.

You need to leave! shouted Aurora once more.

A few dragons seemed to think the same, as some of the Riders rushed to their dragons. Focusing my gaze back onto Anna, I watched her reach out to General Mains. Before anyone could say anything, Anna had grasped a small dagger hidden in her dress. As she reached up with the dagger clenched in her hand, I watched as the blade sliced through the general's throat. Shocked gasps echoed throughout the field, as General Mains' body fell to the ground. Standing at the forest with a smile on her face, Anna raised her head towards the night sky.

"*Gurth na i lúg!*" she shouted. The sound of yells echoed out from the woods, as thousands of rogues ran towards us.

Spinning around, William's grip on my arm tightened. "Get your weapons!" he shouted.

Looking down at me, he gave me a gentle push towards where some dragons were. "Find Aurora!"

Nodding, I ran towards the dragons. Weaving my way through the soldiers, I came to where Aurora should have been, only to find her spot empty. Panicking, I tried to contact her.

"Aurora!" I shouted over the screams of pain.

After a second pause, there was nothing. I couldn't even feel her any more. Panic shot through me as the sounds of running feet came closer. Turning around, I saw rogues flooding the area, with their weapons swinging. I watched as a few soldiers went down, their eyes still open, with blood flowing from their parted lips. I was frozen. I had never seen a man die in front of me before. I had often heard stories of what it was like to see someone die, but actually seeing it was a different story.

My body was frozen. It was almost like I couldn't move. My eyes seemed to be glued to the dead soldier as his eyes bore up into my own, and I knew, if I made it out alive, this man's eyes were going to haunt me in my sleep.

Closing my eyes, I shook my head. Tears threatened to fall as my breath quickened. Licking my lips, I tried to call Aurora.

"Aurora!" I hissed.

Opening my eyes, I looked around the area for a sign of her, but still nothing. A sudden tug on my arm caused my body to react on its own. Pulling my arm out of the tight grasp, I swung my arm around, connecting to a hard cheek.

Gritting my teeth, I prepared myself to fight, but froze when I noticed who I had hit. Looking down at me in shock was Matthew. A dark red mark covered his left cheek, and if the situation were different, I would have smiled. Taking a step away from him, I looked around for a weapon or anything that would help me ward him off. I knew he was the one that had tipped off the Dark Lord of our location; it just had to be.

"Abagail, stop! I'm trying to help you!" Matthew shouted.

Gritting my teeth, I shook my head. "You're working for the Dark King!"

Frowning, Matthew shook his head. "No, it's not me. I've been trying to help you all this time."

"Why should I believe you?" Gritting my teeth, I prepared to fight.

With a frown, Matthew shook his head.

"If you don't believe me, then why don't you ask your mother when you see her next?"

Shocked by his words, I stepped closer. "What?"

Shaking his head, he gripped my arms. "Look, there's no time to explain. You need to go get your weapons!" As he pushed me towards my tent, I contemplated his words. Could I really trust him when all my senses were telling me to run? But if he really isn't the one who tipped King Toban off, then it had to be someone who was close to King Albert. Not having a choice, I nodded, before running off.

Shouts echoed throughout the field as dragons screamed out in pain. Their Riders were getting hurt, and some must even be dying; but right now, there was nothing I could do. I couldn't feel Aurora, nor could I will myself to connect with her. Gritting my teeth, I turned the corner to see Markus fighting off a rogue. The rogue was three times his height, and with every swing from the rogue, I could see Markus struggling. Looking around for some type of weapon, I spotted a discarded sword with blood on the handle. Rushing towards it, I picked it up, before running to Markus.

"Markus, duck!" I shouted. He followed my orders, and I gritted my teeth as I pulled the sword behind me.

"*Rod plural rody.*" The feeling of energy flowed through me as I threw the sword towards the rogue. It hit the rogue on the side of its head with a sickening crack, and I watched the rogue's lifeless body fall to the ground, the sword still sticking from its head. Rushing towards Markus, I grasped his upper arm to help him stand. He had a small cut to his cheek, and the sleeve to his shirt was missing, but overall not a drop of blood was on his armour.

Throwing my arms around his neck, I buried my head into his chest. "Thank god you're okay," he whispered into my hair. Pulling back, he grabbed my hand with his, pulling me towards the fighting. "Come on, this way." Following behind him, I noticed we were heading back towards the field, and as we made our way there, not a single rogue tried to touch us. It was almost like we couldn't be seen. Looking around, I noticed Anna still standing at the edge of the forest, a few rogues guarding her. As I realised where we were going, I tried to pull back, but Markus' grip on my hand only tightened at my attempts.

"Markus, stop!" I shouted out.

Stopping in the middle of the field, he released my hand. He turned towards me, and I noticed his eyes were full of tears. "Are you hurt?" I asked. The sound of a shout behind me caught me off-guard. Gripping my arm, Markus pulled me behind him as a rogue swung its wooden club.

Using his sword to block the rogue's club, Markus kicked the rogue in the stomach, causing it to stagger back. Using the distraction, he swung his sword, slicing through the rogue's neck. I watched as its head rolled to the floor, soon followed by its body. Gripping his arm, I pulled him towards me. I was scared. I didn't understand any of this. I thought the rogues weren't anywhere near the compound. We had been lied to all this time.

"Markus, we need to leave," I yelled.

Turning towards me, his frown deepened. Gripping the top of my shoulder with his free hand, he stepped closer.

"I'm sorry," he whispered, as a tear fell from his eyes.

Frowning up at him, I tried to speak, but the air in my lungs left as the feeling of something sharp entered my stomach. Gasping in shock, I watched as Markus pulled his hand back, taking the sharp object out of me.

Staggering back, I looked down at my stomach. Blood oozed out of the wound, coating my once-crisp white shirt with red. Placing my hands over the wound, I looked up at Markus.

Standing by his side was Anna, a victorious smirk on her face. "Well done, my love."

Turning his face to Anna, he bent down to kiss her.

"Fall back!" someone shouted in the distance.

Sounds around me seemed to blur into a dull echo as my head started to spin. My vision blurred, causing me to fall to my knees, then onto my back. Lying on the grass, I heard dragons scream. Turning my head to the side, I watched

Markus and Anna walk towards the tree-line, their hands clasped together. I couldn't think. I couldn't move. I was frozen as my eyes followed their retreating figures.

Closing my eyes, I took a deep breath, only to regret my actions, as soon after my lungs started to burn. My body felt cold. I didn't feel like I was in control any more. The sound of my name being called fell into my ears as I tried to open my eyes.

William and his dragon landed near me, as Talios shot arrows from Zor's back. Closing my eyes once more, I listened to rushed footsteps as the person neared me.

"Stay with me!" the voice shouted. Groaning, I let my body finally relax. I was tired. All I wanted to do was sleep. As I felt my body being lifted from the hard ground, a soft hum entered my mind. The only thing I could think about was how my mother was going to be now, before everything went dead silent.

The humming in my mind intensified, before a voice seemed to whisper in my ear.

May my dying power heal you, for your time is not now.